A Bonfire Surprise in Stickleback Hollow

The Mysteries of Stickleback Hollow

By C.S. Woolley

A Mightier Than the Sword UK Publication

©2017

1

A Bonfire Surprise in Stickleback Hollow

The Mysteries of Stickleback Hollow

By C. S. Woolley

A Mightier Than the Sword UK Publication

Paperback Edition

Copyright © c. s. woolley 2017

Cover Design © c. s. woolley 2017

For

Szonja

Author's Note

Thanks for taking the time to read *A Bonfire Surprise in Stickleback Hollow*, I hope you enjoy it, there is much more to come in the series if you do!

This book is particular special to me as it contains cricket, one of the things I love most in this world. If you are tempted to yawn and call cricket boring, then you'll miss out on all the fun of the mystery. I do recommend that rather than trying to watch cricket on the TV though, you go out and watch your local team play, or try playing yourself, and find out just how good it is first hand.

The Characters

Lady Sarah Montgomery Baird Watson-Wentworth

The heroine

Brigadier General George Webb-Kneelingroach

Guardian of Lady Sarah and owner of Grangeback

Miss Grace Read

Lady Sarah's lady's maid

Bosworth

The butler

Mrs Bosworth

The housekeeper

Cooky

The cook

Mr Alexander Hunter

A huntsman and groundskeeper of Grangeback

Pattinson

An Akita, Alexander's hunting dog

Constable Arwyn Evans

Policeman in Stickleback Hollow

Doctor Jack Hales

The doctor in Stickleback Hollow

Miss Angela Baker

The seamstress in Stickleback Hollow

Wilson

The innkeeper in Stickleback Hollow

Mrs Emma Wilson

Wife of Wilson and cook at the inn

Mr Henry Cartwright

Former owner of Duffleton Hall

Stanley Baker

Son of Miss Baker

Lee Baker

Son of Miss Baker

Reverend Percy Butterfield

The vicar in Stickleback Hollow

Mr Richard Hales

Son of Doctor Hales

Mr Gordon Hales

Son of Doctor Hales

Lord Daniel Cooper

A gentleman from Duffleton Hall

Mr Stuart Moore

A gentleman of Cheshire

Mr Jake Walker

A gentleman of Cheshire

The Honourable Mr Wilbraham Egerton

Owner of Tatton Park

Mrs Elizabeth Egerton nee Sykes

Wife of Wilbraham

Mr Wilbraham Egerton

Son of Wilbraham & Elizabeth

Mr Thomas Egerton

Son of Wilbraham & Elizabeth

Mrs Charlotte Egerton nee Milner

Wife of Thomas

Mr Edward Christopher Egerton

Son of Wilbraham & Elizabeth

Miss Mary Pierrepont

Fiancée of Edward

Mr Harry Taylor

A gentleman in the employment of John Smith

Mr James Christian

A retired missionary

Mr Mitchell Claydon

An explorer

Miss Millie Roy

A charwoman

Miss Elizabeth Wessex

Fiancée of Lord Daniel Cooper

Mr Johnathen Mullaney

A gentleman of Cheshire

Mrs Abigail Mullaney

A lady of Cheshire

Mrs Ruth Cooper

Mother of Mr Daniel Cooper

Mr Gregory Kitts

A gentleman of Cheshire

Mr Samuel Jones

A gentleman of Cheshire

Mr Luke Lumb

A gentleman of the Antipodes

Mr Timothy Wood

A gentleman of Cheshire

Mr Richard Ball

A gentleman of Cheshire

Mr Michael Hutton

A gentleman of Cheshire

Mr Joseph Blatherwick

A gentleman of Cheshire

Mr S. Carter

The butcher

Mr Anthony Herridge

A farmer

Mr Ross Pick

A Greengrocer

Mr Andrew Christopher

The verger

Lord Joshua St. Vincent

A young lord in the employ of Lady Carol-Ann

Mr Callum St. Vincent

A young gentleman in the employ of Lady Carol-Ann

John Smith

An Alias

Lady Carol-Ann Margaret de Mandeville, Duchess of Aumale and Montagu

The villain

The Opposition

Yorkshire

C A Aubrey-Smith

Leslie O'Brian 'Chuck' Fleetwood-Smith

Tobias Skelton 'Roly' Roland-Jones

Colin Ingleby-Mckenzie

Daniel Bell-Drummond

Rory Hamilton-Brown

Thomas Kohler Cadmore

Major Hesketh Vernon Hesketh-Pritchard

Alec Douglas-Hulme

Robin Martin-Jenkins

Sir Spencer Cecil Brabazon Ponsonby-Fane

Nathan Caulter-Niall

Henry Levesen Gower

Staffordshire

The Honourable Frederic Ponsonby, The 6th Earl of Bessborough

The Reverend David Sheperd

Sir Pelham Warner

Sir Gabby Allen

Sir Richard Hadley

Sir Garfield St Alban Sobers

Sir Don Bradman

Lord Harris of Kent

Baron Michael Colin Cowdrey of Tonbridge

Baron Learie Nicholas Constantine

Lord Martin Bladen Hawke

Sir Tim O'Brien, 3rd Baronet of Merrion Square and Boris-in-Ossory

Lancashire

Basil D'Oliveria

William Edrich

George Headley

William Gunn

William Root

Denis Compton

Joe Hardstaff

Peter Hearn

Derek Walker

Mattheus Hendrik Wessels

George Mann

Benjamin Caine Hollieoake

Stephen Michael Gatting

Chapter 1

The definition of a foreigner is someone who doesn't understand cricket. At least that was how the Reverend Percy Butterfield defined foreigners. When your three main interests in life are cricket, the railway and the church, the way in which you view the world is rather oversimplified.

From St. Stephen's Day until March, the only thing that occupied the reverend's mind was the upcoming cricket season.

It wasn't anything great to speak of, a competition between the local villages that ran from April to August. It had been started by the ladies in one of the neighbouring villages in remembrance of their husbands who had died in the Napoleonic Wars. The men had been keen on the sport, and it seemed like a fitting memorial, much more so than a plaque on a wall.

As time had gone on, more and more people had become interested in the game and the grand tournament to open the season had been introduced just a few years before.

The grand tournament was the champion teams from the village leagues in Cheshire, Lancashire, Yorkshire and Staffordshire competing against one another to be named County Champions before the next season began.

It brought people from all over the four counties to watch them play over the few weeks that the grand tournament was held.

The location changed from year to year. Whichever team had the highest run score for the season hosted the grand tournament. It had been several years since Stickleback Hollow had played host to the event, but thanks to the bowling of Doctor Hales and the batting of Mr Timothy Wood, this year the grand tournament was coming to the village in Cheshire.

So it fell to Reverend Percy Butterfield to organise the event. This meant that his mind was more occupied with the sport than normal, which most of the village hadn't believed was possible.

He had arranged lodgings for each of the teams and had Brigadier George Webb-Kneelingroach's footmen employed to maintain the cricket pitch during the tournament.

Miss Baker, Cooky and Mrs Mullaney had been placed in charge of the refreshments for the matches, and the brigadier had agreed to pay for it all.

And though generally it was only the reverend that was excited about the sport, with the Grand Tournament on its way, the entire village was becoming more and more obsessed with the sport.

Lady Sarah had never seen anything of cricket when she had lived in India. It was played there, but rather than spending her time watching the games, she was often engaged in more active pursuits.

Her first experience of the game came when Mr Hunter took her to watch the Cheshire team train. The Cheshire team had gone through some changes as Doctor Hales had chosen to retire from the game.

As it had been his bowling that had delivered the Grand Tournament to Stickleback Hollow, it had been nothing short of scandalous when he had chosen to retire at the end of the season.

Mr Alexander Hunter had been a good bowler

during his school days, but he had never shown much interest in playing for the county when he returned to Stickleback Hollow.

Now that Doctor Hales had retired, Mr Hunter's bowling talents were required, and he was hardly in a position to refuse, especially with the matches set to take place on the grounds of Grangeback.

It had been several months since Mr Hunter had discovered the truth about his parentage and things had been somewhat strained between himself and his father, Brigadier George Webb-Kneelingroach.

The brigadier had raised Alex after his mother had died, but it had only been three months since George had told Mr Hunter that he was his father. In those three months, the two men had barely spoken, and Alex's presence at Grangeback had been conspicuous by its absence.

Lady Sarah had spent most of her time trying to heal the rift between the two men, but Mr Hunter had needed time away from his father to deal with the myriad of emotions that he felt at being lied to for so many years.

After two months, Lady Sarah had given up trying

to get the two men to talk to each other; instead, she had taken to asking Mr Hunter about cricket. It was difficult for the hunter to explain the finer points of the game to the young lady whilst sat in front of the fire in the lodge, so he opted to take her to the practise sessions that the reverend had organised.

"Who are the men that are standing around over there?" Sarah asked when the pair arrived at the cricket pavilion that stood on the outskirts of the village.

"Mr Herridge works on a farm on the Grangeback estate, he helps with improving our bowlers," Alex explained as he pointed at the tall man who was sat on the pavilion steps.

"He doesn't play?" Sarah asked.

"No, he can't run. He had polio when he was very young. It's a miracle he can still walk, but he gets tired very quickly and spends a lot of time in pain," Alex explained.

"How can he work on a farm then?" Sarah asked.

"He's very good with animals; he takes care of the horses that are used to plough and trains the sheepdogs," Alex replied.

"Who are the others?" Sarah asked.

"Mr Pick is the greengrocer, and before he got shot in the knee, he was the best batsman that the county had to offer. He was trying to stop some men from robbing the jewellers in Chester when he got shot, so now, he tries to help impart his knowledge to us," Mr Hunter smiled.

"Did he stop the robbers?" Sarah frowned.

"He did, it was a few years before our police force was introduced, so it was the town watch that came to take the robbers away," Alex explained.

"Who is the third man, the one stood talking to the reverend?" Sarah asked.

"That's Mr Christopher, he's the new verger, and he's as obsessed with cricket as the reverend by all reports," Alex grinned.

"Then the two of them should get along like a house on fire," Sarah smiled back.

The Cheshire team had been selected from villages across the county. There were a great deal of talented cricketers to choose from, a problem that the reverend was happy to have. It meant that if injury or illness side-lined a member of the team, there were still a number of men that could be called upon to fill empty places in the team.

So great was the reputation of the Grand Tournament that all the young gentlemen across all four counties had been given leave by the universities to play in it.

The final first eleven squad for Cheshire was as follows:

Mr Richard Ball

Mr S. Carter

Mr Joseph Blatherwick

Mr Jonathan Mullaney

Mr Gordon Hales (c)

Mr Michael Hutton

Mr Luke Lumb

Mr James Christian (w)

Mr Stuart Moore

Mr Gregory Kitts

Mr Alexander Hunter

The reserves for the team included Mr Mitchell Claydon, Mr Thomas Egerton, Mr Edward Egerton, Mr Richard Hales, Mr Samuel Jones, Mr Timothy Wood and Mr

Jake Walker.

"Watch us practise, and when we are done, you can ask any questions that you can think of," Mr Hunter said as he left Sarah at the boundary rope with Pattinson to sit with her for company.

Sarah watched the team practice for several hours, and at the end of it, she was no closer to knowing anything about the sport or the questions that she needed to ask than she had been at the start of it.

"I feel that this could be a very long tournament," she sighed to Pattinson. The dog cocked his head and whined in reply.

Chapter 2

"My lady, a letter has arrived for you. The envelope is very faded though," Grace greeted Sarah as she returned to Grangeback that evening.

Grace had been employed as Sarah's lady's maid shortly before Christmas, and it had been something of a shock for the young maid.

Lady Sarah was far from the conventional lady of breeding in the upper echelons of society. When Grace had been hired by the brigadier, she had expected a lady of temperance and patience with a quiet and demure demeanour.

What she had in a mistress was a woman that was quite different. Lady Sarah was a stark contrast to the stereotype that Grace had expected. Lady Sarah loved the outdoors; she seemed to go searching for adventure and danger instead of searching for a husband.

The glitter of high society held no draw for Lady Montgomery Baird Watson-Wentworth, in fact, she found it rather tiresome. Her wardrobe was influenced more by the fashions of India than the fashions of London. Her ladyship spent more time riding across the countryside and visiting with people that most of the gentry would consider beneath her station than she invested in learning to play musical instruments or learning needlepoint.

Grace was convinced that Lady Sarah had never been instructed in the finer points of what was expected of ladies in British society, and the brigadier didn't seem inclined to force any form of expectation to conform onto the shoulders of his ward and heir.

This had meant that Grace had to put up with a great deal of horror and turmoil in serving her mistress – at least horror and turmoil as far as a sheltered lady's maid was concerned.

The kidnapping and imprisonment of Lady Sarah in a lunatic asylum by the henchmen of the woman that had murdered Lady Sarah's parents had been Grace's introduction to the peculiar insanities of life at Grangeback.

Since the circus had left Stickleback Hollow at the start of the year, life had fallen into a much more tolerable rhythm for the lady's maid. There had been a small handful of strange occurrences and moments when the brigadier, Mr Hunter and Constable Evans had acted in a manner that suggested danger was lurking close at hand. But all of these had seemed to be nothing more than false alarms and the overly-cautious nature of men intent on protecting someone that was important to them.

Yet, when the letter had arrived for Lady Sarah that morning, Grace had felt a rather tight knot form in her stomach.

Something told her that the letter was an ill-omen and that its contents would bring nothing but misery upon the household.

"It's only a letter," Sarah said when she saw the severe expression on Grace's face.

"I'm sorry, my lady?" Grace replied.

"The way you look, one would be forgiven for thinking it was really a basket of vipers," Lady Sarah smiled.

"My apologies, I have left it on your dressing table," Grace said, failing to sound any happier about the arrival of the letter.

"I think you have been cooped up at the house for

too long, Grace. Have one of the footmen invite Miss Roy to the house for breakfast tomorrow. We'll all go into Chester for the day and order new gowns for the ball we are giving at the end of the Grand Tournament," Lady Sarah said as she gently took Grace by the arm and walked her through the house.

"Very well, my lady," Grace forced a smile across her lips, but she couldn't rid herself of the sinking feeling that was beginning to make her feel sick.

Sarah left Grace at the bottom of the stairs and made her way up to her rooms alone. She felt tired after spending the day being educated in cricket, but for the hours she had spent watching the men, she was still none-the-wiser about the finer points of the game.

If it hadn't been for Mr Hunter playing in the tournament, she wouldn't care that she didn't understand the game. But as it was important to Alex, she wanted to at least be able to understand the game, even if she was convinced that she would never be able to enjoy it.

The arrival of a letter was something of a welcome relief, though she couldn't imagine who was writing to her.

She entered her rooms and went to examine the

envelope. The handwriting looked somewhat familiar and but the accuracy of the address on the envelope concerned her.

The only people that would be writing to her would all be in India or her family in London – though she suspected that anything her family had to say would be sent by messenger or telegram.

Her friends and family acquaintances in India had been given the London address of her aunt, and her aunt had been given strict instructions to redirect any post that arrived for Sarah.

This letter hadn't been redirected.

Lady Sarah picked up the letter off the dressing table and sat down on the sofa before she opened it and began to read.

She read through the letter twice before she set it down on the table and thought carefully about its contents.

Sarah,

It has been a long time since I last saw you, but we parted as friends. As your friend, I need to warn you, Mr

Harry Taylor is in England, and he will do whatever it takes to serve the needs of his employer. He is not the idiot he pretends to be, nor is he by any means harmless or helpless.

Be careful.

Samit

Her first instinct was to burn the letter. She hated the way that her friends reacted when they thought she was in danger and them discovering such a letter had been sent to her would do nothing to discourage their rather heavy-handed form of protection.

On the other hand, not telling them that Mr Taylor was reportedly in the country also put them at risk.

The date on the letter told Sarah that it had been written months ago. She sat and thought for a while about what she should do.

The length of time that it had taken for the letter to arrive and the lack of incident over the last few months made Sarah think that there was a possibility that Harry

Taylor was no longer in the country.

She resolved to hide the letter in the bottom drawer of her dressing table and quietly try to discover if anyone had seen anything of Mr Taylor.

If it proved that he was still in the country, then she would show the letter to Mr Hunter, George and Constable Evans.

When Sarah came down for dinner that evening, she didn't mention the letter and Grace didn't ask about it. The lady's maid kept a careful eye on her ladyship, but knew that discretion was the better part of valour and nothing good could be gained from bringing up the letter in front of the brigadier before she knew what it was about it.

Nothing was said about the letter that evening, nor was it mentioned when Miss Millie Roy arrived for breakfast the following day.

When the plan for the day was explained to the brigadier, he insisted that the ladies take some form of escort with them.

None of the footmen could be spared from their duties, so Mrs Bosworth went down into the village to enlist the Baker boys, Stanley and Lee.

Neither of the boys were particularly old or sensible, but the women in the company of the teenagers would be enough to keep the pickpockets and minor criminals away.

"I'll send for Mr Hunter, he'll have to go with you," George dithered after Mrs Bosworth had departed.

"George, we'll be fine. We're going to one shop. The carriage can stop outside the shop, and then we only have the distance across the pavement to cross," Sarah soothed.

By the time Mrs Bosworth returned with the Baker boys, the brigadier had begrudgingly agreed that the women could go into the city with only the two boys as an escort.

Chapter 3

Miss Baker was a talented seamstress, but she was very busy in the spring. Not only had the brigadier tasked her with making spring and summer clothing for Lady Sarah, but the families of the neighbour also brought their trade to her door.

On top of this, Miss Baker was also the leatherworker in Stickleback Hollow, which meant that she had work from everyone from farmers to the great houses that she needed to get through.

This meant that there was no way that she could make gowns for the Grand Tournament ball as well. It also meant that if there was any way of keeping her sons, Stanley and Lee, out of her shop and out of trouble, she was going to jump at it.

It was due to this second reason that Stanley and Lee Baker were quickly sent back to Grangeback with Mrs Bosworth. Neither of the boys were particularly happy with the task they had been given as shopping escorts, but they were not going to disobey their mother.

Stanley and Lee Baker were not Miss Baker's biological sons. When they had been born, Miss Baker had found them in an alley in Chester. She had taken them to the city watch, but their parents couldn't be traced.

The two babies were set to be bound for the Roodee workhouse, but Miss Baker had refused to allow that to happen. She already had an established business as a seamstress in Stickleback Hollow and could more than afford to bring up the boys.

The workhouse had no objection to her keeping the babies, after the brigadier and Reverend Butterfield had written a letter about Miss Baker's character to them, so the boys had been adopted.

This act of charity and compassion on the part of Miss Baker had given her an even better standing in the community and had led to an increase in her business amongst the households in Cheshire that wished to be associated with an individual of such good Christian morals.

Both Stanley and Lee knew that they were adopted, but they also knew that Miss Angela Baker loved them both as much, if not more, than a biological mother would have. She treated them well, and both boys felt secure in the knowledge that no matter how much trouble they got into and caused, Miss Baker had chosen to love them and would always love them.

They also knew they would be punished if they disobeyed her, so the boys had gone with Mrs Bosworth, though they were somewhat sullen as they climbed into the carriage with Miss Roy, Miss Read and Lady Montgomery Baird Watson-Wentworth.

The city of Chester was a few miles from Stickleback Hollow, so the journey in the carriage took a while, even after they reached the main road into the city.

Stanley and Lee sat pouting in the carriage as it rolled along and stared out of the windows. Lady Sarah was lost in thought about the letter she had received from Samit, but Grace and Millie weren't affected by the quiet demeanour of their fellow passengers.

The two young girls chatted away as the carriage lurched along. Since Lady Sarah and Grace had investigated the disappearance of Millie's small pearl broach, friendship had blossomed easily between the women..

There was a lot about the young charwoman that begged questioning, but neither Lady Sarah nor Grace had pressed the issue with her.

Instead, Grace and Millie had become very good friends, something that had allowed Lady Sarah space enough to spend time on her own with Mr Hunter.

The drive into the city meant that the two girls had plenty of time to talk about the local news and ask each other questions about what had happened since they last met.

By the time the carriage stopped outside the windows of Mrs Morgan's Gowns and Lady's Apparel, the two girls had said discussed all the village news and even exhausted the topic of conversation.

The two boys were the first to leap out of the carriage and led the three women into the shop.

Mrs Morgan was a woman who was used to charming her clientele and wasted no time in ingratiating herself into Lady Sarah's good graces.

"My lady, how wonderful to see you! How can I assist you today?" Mrs Morgan smiled at Lady Sarah.

"We're here for three gowns for the Grand

Tournament ball," Lady Sarah replied as she looked at the reams of material that lined the shelves behind the bespoke counter.

"Three, my lady?" Mrs Morgan sounded surprised.

"Yes, one for myself, one for Miss Read and the other for Miss Roy; all on my account of course," Lady Sarah smiled.

"Excellent, come, ladies, tell me what you have in mind. We'll choose the fabric, the style and I shall take the measurements I need," Mrs Morgan said as he clapped her hands with delight.

Grace and Millie looked at one another with confused expressions on their faces.

"Excuse me, my lady, but neither of us is going to the ball," Grace whispered.

"Of course you are," Sarah replied, "you expect me to go on my own?"

The ladies spent a few hours making all the arrangements for their gowns. Mrs Morgan sent for the cobbler so that he could make shoes to match the gowns for the ladies and the jeweller came to discuss pieces that the ladies might want to wear as well.

Stanley and Lee fell asleep after only an hour of the ladies chatter about what they were going to wear. Miss Roy seemed to be far more knowledgeable than a simple charwoman should have been about fabrics, shoes and jewellery; and she also had a surprising knowledge about the most fashionable styles of gowns in London.

The jeweller had excitedly written down the pieces of jewellery that the ladies wanted, and the cobbler was measuring Lady Sarah's feet when the door to the shop opened, and four men walked in.

It was unusual enough for gentlemen to be in Mrs Morgan's shop, but these four men were as far from gentlemen as you could possibly get.

They were rough-looking men with clothing that reeked of beer and urine. Stanley and Lee were both still asleep, but had they been awake there was very little that they could have done in order to prevent what happened next.

Two of the men seized hold of Millie, and the other two grabbed Grace. The jeweller and Mrs Morgan were all slow to react. Lady Sarah tried to get up to bar the path of the men to the door, but the cobbler was in her way. By the time the lady had managed to push past the cobbler, the two women were already on the street, both screaming for help.

People stared as Lady Sarah rushed into the street, flanked by the two Baker boys. Sarah was fumbling with her purse as she came through the door and eventually pulled out her pistol.

The men were only a few steps away from her; the struggling women were making it difficult for the men to get away quickly.

"Let them go, or I will shoot." Lady Sarah shouted. People were coming out of shops to see what all the screaming was about and the sound of whistles coming closer told the four men that they were running out of time.

Stanley and Lee Baker saw the two men holding Millie hesitate and rushed at them, shouting. The two boys went for the legs of the men, causing them to trip, freeing Millie. The men fought to try and free themselves, but the Baker boys clung on for dear life.

With Millie free, she scrambled away from the men, and Sarah fired her pistol at one of the men holding Grace. The bullet struck him in the arm, causing him to let go of

Grace and cry out in pain.

Sarah began to reload her pistol. Grace was scratching at the man who held her with her free hand. The sound of the policemen approaching grew louder, and the last man standing gave up.

He waited until the police were in sight and pushed Grace into them. People were crowding the street now, and chaos seemed to have erupted as more policemen arrived. The last man slipped away through the crowd as the police handcuffed the other three and took reports of what had happened from the bystanders and Lady Sarah's entourage.

Grace and Millie were taken into Mrs Morgan's shop to recover from the shock. Sarah stood watching the three men being taken away by the police and tried to work out why anyone would want to try and take a charwoman and a lady's maid; and who had known where they were.

Stanley and Lee Baker were hailed as heroes by the police, and a few people from the crowd rewarded the boys with half crowns and small bags of humbugs.

By the time the party returned to Stickleback Hollow, the news of the attempted kidnapping had already circulated the village three times.

The brigadier and Mr Hunter both waited anxiously at Grangeback, along with Constable Evans, Doctor and Gordon Hales.

Curtains twitched as the carriage trundled through the village. The carriage didn't stop as it went through Stickleback Hollow, instead the driver made for Grangeback.

The sound of the carriage approaching the house brought the four men, along with the household staff out into the gathering darkness to greet the three women and two boys.

"Millie!" Gordon cried as he saw the girl being helped out of the carriage. He ran over and wrapped his arms around as she burst into tears.

"Grace! Oh, dear me!" Mrs Bosworth fussed as Grace followed Millie out of the carriage. The housekeeper put her arm around Grace's shoulders and steered her into the house with Cooky joining the pair to cluck and coo over the lady's maid.

"Stanley, Lee, come with me," the brigadier instructed the boys as they got out of the carriage. The doctor quietly made his way to check on Millie.

Sarah was the last to descend from the carriage. Mr Hunter waited on the steps of the great house for the lady to reach him.

"Are you alright?" he asked gently as she stood next to him.

"No," she replied softly, "I need to make arrangements for Miss Roy to stay here tonight and for the Baker Boys to be escorted home."

"When George is finished with the boys, I'll make sure they get home. Do you want me to come back?" Alex asked in a low voice.

"Yes," Sarah said as she looked at him with a worried expression.

"What is it?" Alex frowned.

"I have a letter you should see," Sarah sighed before continuing into the house.

Chapter 4

Sarah stayed awake until Alex returned to the house. She was sat up in bed and had the letter from Samit in her hand.

"How was Miss Baker?" Sarah asked as Mr Hunter slipped into her room.

"She was shaken, but glad the boys were back safe and sound. She did seem to be more concerned about how you, Miss Read and Miss Roy were," Alex sighed as he sat down on the edge of the bed and shook his head.

"At least she wasn't in the same state as Cooky and Mrs Bosworth. After the doctor had looked at Millie and Grace, he had to calm both of them down with sedatives," Sarah smiled to herself.

"They're right to be worried. Going into Chester shouldn't have put the five of you in danger," Mr Hunter looked over at Sarah with a serious expression.

"What do you expect me to do? Stay in this room with the curtains drawn and the doors locked?" Sarah asked churlishly.

"No, of course not," Alex replied and reached out to take her hand, "I just want you to be safe. We all do," he gave her a slight smile.

"Here, you should read this," Sarah handed Alex the note instead of taking his hand. Mr Hunter took the letter and read it through slowly. When he was finished, he read it again.

"How do you know this Samit?" Alex asked.

"He was a friend in India, he's one of the natives, but we played together as children. Of all the people I know, I trust him more than most – present company accepted," Sarah replied as she hugged her knees to her chest.

Mr Hunter looked at Lady Sarah as he weighed his next words carefully. He had known Harry Taylor since his school days and there besides the same torture as other boys that he had subjected Alex to at the time, there was nothing about his behaviour that suggested he was anything other than the spoilt son of a rich man.

He didn't know what to make of the note. Nothing he knew of Harry told him that he'd be able to survive anywhere except in large stately homes where servants took care of most of his needs. The idea that he was lurking somewhere seemed to be outrageous for the hunter to entertain.

"What are you thinking of?" Sarah asked, disturbing Alex's train of thought.

"Are you sure that he can be trusted? From what I know of Mr Taylor, there is no possibility that he could remain in the county without one of our acquaintances knowing where he was," Alex frowned.

"Unless he is being hidden by others that work for Lady de Mandeville," Sarah replied.

"There is that," Mr Hunter sighed and ran his hand through his hair, "Danger seems to follow you wherever you go," he said as he handed her back the letter.

"Only since I came to England. In India, I never had to deal with anything like this." Sarah replied as she took the letter and got up to put it away in her dressing table.

"You really miss it, don't you?" Alex asked as he looked at her, standing in front of the mirror.

"India? Yes, but mostly because I miss my family. My mother was a wonderful singer, though she couldn't play an instrument. She made sure that I learned to play the piano so that she had someone to accompany her when we weren't at parties," Sarah smiled sadly at the memory.

"You should hold onto those kinds of memories, they help. Keep the good and leave the bad," Mr Hunter said softly.

"Do you think that Mr Taylor had something to do with the men that tried to take Millie and Grace?" Sarah asked as she turned back to face Mr Hunter.

"If your friend from India is right, then it is a distinct possibility. But surely those men would have tried to take you, not Miss Roy and Miss Read if Harry was involved," Alex shrugged.

"Perhaps, it could be something to do with Millie or Grace's family though," Sarah sighed with frustration as she walked back to the bed and sat next to Alex. The hunter slipped his arm around her waist as she leant her head on his shoulder.

"Maybe tonight is not the best time to think about all of this. You've had a long day, and you need sleep," Mr Hunter said gently.

"I don't think I can sleep after today," Sarah said drowsily.

"If it helps, I can explain the value of a good forward defensive stroke to you for at least an hour," Alex grinned down at her.

"That might not help, I'm beginning to find cricket quite interesting," Sarah smiled back.

o-o-o

As the tournament grew closer, more stories about previous games and the history behind some of the nicknames amongst the team began to emerge. This only served to fuel the excitement that was growing in the village.

Sarah had begun to understand some of the basics of the game, but a lot of the nuances of the game still escaped her.

George and Doctor Hales had spent the first two nights after the incident locked in George's study talking about what effect it might have on the Grand Tournament and how best to keep the ladies safe.

To prevent strangers from tramping around Grangeback after what had happened to the ladies in Chester, the members of the Cheshire were given rooms at Grangeback.

On the third day, Chief Constable Captain Thomas Jonnes Smith came to Grangeback to speak to Millie, Grace and Sarah about the men. There was something strange in his countenance that neither Constable Evans nor Mr Hunter could explain.

The man was normally a blustering figure that expected everyone to respond to him as his troops had in his military days. During his visit to Grangeback he was rather demure and seemed to be lost in thought.

Neither Alex nor Arwyn were in a position where they could question the Chief Constable about his demeanour, but it did leave both men resolved to keep the three women close at hand at all times. After all, when a man like Captain Jonnes Smith was worried, there was certainly something to be concerned about.

Since then, no matter where the three women were. Millie had been moved into Grace's room so that she wasn't in the village on her own and when she went to work as a charwoman, two of the footmen from Grangeback went with her.

Lady Sarah was forbidden from leaving the grounds of the house until the brigadier was satisfied that it was safe for her to do so, and with Sarah confined to Grangeback, Grace was also.

Four days had passed since the attempted abduction of Millie and Grace, and though both girls seemed to have recovered from the shock of it, Arwyn and Alex were both more than a little unsettled about the incident.

However, neither man had much time to dwell on the event as the teams for the Grand Tournament arrived. Each squad consisted of at least thirteen men, all of whom had to be accommodated as well as those that had travelled to Stickleback Hollow to watch the Grand Tournament.

The men of the Cheshire cricket squad moved into Grangeback creating a great deal of upheaval in the household, at least as far as Mrs Bosworth was concerned.

The strange mixture of gentry and commoners was something that had the housekeeper tutting to herself as she marched up and down the corridors of the great house. Bosworth kept his own counsel on the matter, but the old butler didn't seem to be too upset by the presence of all of the brigadier's guests.

Cooky could be heard singing in the kitchen as she merrily prepared dinner for the first night. It had been a long time since the house had so many guests for her to cook for and the challenge of filling the table brought joy to her heart.

The maids were scolded for giggling as Mr Blatherwick, Mr Moore and Mr Kitts swaggered down to the drawing room. Mrs Bosworth didn't approve of that kind of behaviour from the staff. They were there to see to the needs of the household, not disgrace themselves and lose their honour to young gentlemen with little regard for those they considered beneath them.

Due to the size of Grangeback, there were more than enough rooms to cater for the eighteen men that had descended on the house. The brigadier and Lady Sarah had rooms in the East Wing of the house; the servants' quarters were in the attic rooms of East Wing which left the rooms of the West Wing for the cricket team to occupy.

Each man was given his own room and instruction from Bosworth that they could go anywhere except the East Wing.

"Why, what's in the East Wing?" Mr Jones had asked.

"It's forbidden," had been the only response that

Bosworth had been willing to give.

Though Arwyn was not in the cricket team, he also took up residence in the West Wing, hoping to provide the ladies with a little more protection and allowing him to be more vigilant.

The chief inspector had sent Constable Cantello and Constable McIntyre to help police Stickleback as preparations for the tournament were in their final stage, with the promise of more men to be sent to keep the peace when it began.

The two constables moved into the police house in Arwyn's stead, and Constable Evans trusted the pair of them to take care of the village whilst he watched the estate.

Wilson's inn was playing host to the Lancashire team; the men had requested berths at the inn as they claimed to play better after a few pints of best bitter. Whether that was true or the bitter simply made them believe that they were playing better was a matter of opinion, but Wilson had been more than happy to grant the request; especially when the brigadier had assured him that the bill for the Lancashire squad should be sent to

Grangeback.

The Egerton family at Tatton Park was more than happy to provide the Yorkshire squad with lodgings for the tournament. Thomas and Edward reported that the team had arrived in full before they had left and that they had been managed to learn some useful information about the condition of some of the Yorkshire players.

The Staffordshire squad had been offered accommodation at Duffleton Hall as titled personages, it had been agreed that Lord Daniel Cooper was the most appropriate host – especially since many of the men had known him since he was born.

With the teams quartered in separate locations, there was ample room for each team to practise without interruption. The Lancashire side trained on the village green in Stickleback Hollow, with one of the constables in attendance to ensure that no one bothered them.

The other cricket teams had more than enough room on each of the estates that they were guests upon to practise without fear of disruption.

Dinner was an interesting affair at Grangeback that first evening. The Reverend Percy Butterfield had been invited to dine with them each evening as though he wanted to stay at the manor with the rest of the team; he had to tend to the spiritual needs of the parish instead of simply indulging his passion for cricket.

Mr S. Carter, the butcher from Stickleback Hollow, sat in stoic silence. He was a man that wasn't known to talk much, but during dinner, it was a little disconcerting for those that weren't used to him.

To try and avoid and unnecessary awkwardness, the brigadier had Mr Carter sit between Doctor Hales and the reverend so that the two men could talk about cricket across the butcher and make it seem like he was being sociable.

George sat at the head of the table with Sarah at the far end, opposite him. To his right was the doctor, the butcher and the reverend. Alex sat to Sarah's right with Thomas, and Edward sat to her left. The rest of the team were spread around the table, though Gordon Hales had made a point of sitting next to Millie.

Grace was the only one absent from dinner as she was feeling unwell. Doctor Hales had been to check on her before dinner and was happy to report that she was merely exhausted from the stress of the ordeal in Chester.

Mrs Bosworth took her some dinner and sat with the lady's maid for a while. Grace lay and listened to the housekeeper, expressing her disapproval at the house being full of young wastrels. Though she had no riposte when Grace pointed out that Mrs Bosworth didn't consider them to be wastrels when they were on the cricket pitch.

When Mrs Bosworth took the tray down to the kitchen, dinner was over. Millie was on her way to bed, and the men were moving to the billiard room for brandy and cigars. Sarah and Alex lingered in the hallway for a moment before Mr Hunter followed the rest of the men.

"You need to be careful, my lady," Mrs Bosworth warned as she came down the final flight of stairs and passed the heir of Grangeback.

"What do you mean?" Sarah asked, trying to sound as off-hand as she could.

"You and Mr Hunter haven't been as discreet as you would like to think. Though only I seem to be aware of your late-night assignations, with so many in the house, it will only be a matter of time until someone else notices," Mrs Bosworth gently warned her.

"We're not -" Sarah began, but Mrs Bosworth fixed

her with a stare that told caused the young lady to falter.

"Until the brigadier has recognised Mr Hunter as his son publically, any relationship between the two of you will be a scandal. If it comes to light that you and Mr Hunter have explored the carnal side of nature together, then it would be -" Mrs Bosworth allowed her voice to trail off and patted Sarah's arm, "Just be careful."

Chapter 5

Wilson's inn was far livelier than Mr Hunter could ever remember. Wilson had taken on extra help in order to keep the inn running smoothly whilst the Lancashire cricket team was staying there.

With Arwyn, Thomas and Edward at Grangeback, Mr Hunter felt it was safe enough to leave Sarah in the house whilst he went down to the village to try and observe the daily comings and goings.

Constable Evans and the hunter had agreed to take it in turns to visit the village on a daily basis to look for any signs that Mr Harry Taylor might still be in the area or listen out for any news of him.

After Sarah had shown the letter to Alex, he had spoken to Arwyn about it the next morning. Both men had agreed that as unlikely that it seemed that Mr Taylor was still in the area, it was better to be safe than sorry.

Mr Hunter sat in the inn listening to snatches of conversations to see if he could learn anything interesting.

There was some discussion amongst the cricket players about Harry. He had played for Staffordshire in previous years and had forged a reputation as a legendary batsman that caused every bowler to wake up at night in cold sweats.

The conversations had all been discussing his absence from the side this year and theorising what effect that would have on the tournament.

Most of the bowlers seemed relieved at the prospect of not bowling against Harry in the tournament; a few mentioned that it was a shame he wasn't in the side and speculated about why he wasn't competing.

None of this helped Mr Hunter learn whether Samit had been right in his letter to Lady Sarah, but it would at least make the tournament a little easier for the Cheshire, Lancashire and Yorkshire sides.

The trips into Stickleback Hollow also gave Mr Hunter time to think, a luxury that he had been missing in the last few months.

Since the first night he had spent making love to Lady Sarah, she was all that he could think about. He spent as much time with her as he could, and when the two were apart, he thought about her constantly.

He had never understood before what it was about women that made otherwise rational men completely lose all perspective and act like fools. Since their first adventure together in Chester, Alex had not only understood but surrendered to being a fool for Sarah, regardless of how she treated him.

Yet he was still torn about how her reputation would be affected when their affair became public. The more he thought about George's offer to recognise him as his son, and elevate him to the status of a gentleman, the more Alex felt he should agree.

George had always been like a father to him, so the idea of recognising him as his father was not one that was beyond his imagination. What held him back was how angry he felt at the secret being kept for so long.

Mr Hunter could understand the brigadier's reticence to admit to fathering an illegitimate child when his wife was still alive. But in the wake of her death and that of Alex's mother, all either of them had left was each other. Rather than recognise him as his son, George had sent Alex away to school where he was miserable and bullied by the sons of gentlemen for not being one of them.

These same gentlemen had come to accept Alex as one of their own after he had rescued a handful of them from a rather dangerous situation in Chester, but that had not been until years after Alex had left the school in favour of learning to be the groundskeeper at Grangeback.

But it had made Mr Hunter certain that he never wanted to be counted as a member of that social sphere, but for Sarah's sake, he would be willing to put up with it.

Mrs Bosworth had been waiting for Alex when the gentlemen had finished their nightcap in the billiard room. She had told him that she knew about his relationship with Sarah and that he needed to be more careful.

Mr Hunter didn't say anything as Mrs Bosworth spoke to him, but he knew that she was right. He loved Sarah and didn't want to see her disgraced. Before he left for Stickleback Hollow, Alex and Sarah had agreed to spend their nights apart and less time together during the day.

Mr Hunter spent three hours at the inn and learned nothing about whether Harry Taylor was in the area. He said a gruff goodbye to Wilson and stepped out onto the village street.

The warmth of spring was in the air and a welcome

feeling after the cold winter months, especially with the approaching cricket tournament.

Alex set off down the road, heading towards the different shops in the square to see if the proprietors had any news to share. He saw Constable Cantello in the street and nodded to him.

Though he hadn't spent much time with the constable, Mr Hunter liked him well enough, and Arwyn spoke more highly of his character than anyone else that the hunter knew.

Everything seemed to be perfect and peaceful in the village. People were as bright as the day around them, shaking off the winter blues.

"Good morning, Mr Hunter, how are things up at Grangeback?" Constable Cantello asked.

"Mrs Bosworth is muttering about the number of guests, Cooky is enjoying cooking for a full house and cricket is the only topic of conversation that anyone is interested in," Alex grinned at the policeman.

"Well, that's good to hear," Constable Cantello rocked on the balls of his feet.

"How are things here in the village?" Mr Hunter

asked.

"Much quieter than in Chester. Not seen hide nor hair of a pickpocket anywhere about. It's the kind of place that Sergeant Burt would be bored in," the constable replied.

"Let us hope it stays quiet," Alex murmured, more to himself than the policeman.

"How do you rate your chances of winning the tournament?" the constable asked.

"I'd like to think we'll win, but as you know, with cricket, anything can happen," Alex sighed and shook his head.

"True enough. I can remember three years ago when everyone was convinced that Yorkshire were going to walk away with the tournament prize. Then they went and lost every match. Harry Ogden had come up from the Great Wen and made a fortune taking bets," Constable Cantello laughed to himself.

"Where there is money to be made from gambling, you can be certain that Harry Ogden or his boys won't be too far away," Alex replied.

"Well, I should get back to my rounds," the constable

nodded to Mr Hunter and continued on down the street. Alex looked after him with a wry smile and made his way towards Miss Baker's shop.

As he reached the door to the shop, two rather large men pushed their way past him. The hunter was a tall man with broad shoulders and not short on muscle, but the size of these two men made him look almost small by comparison.

Aside from their size, there was nothing unusual about the two men.

"Good morning, Miss Baker," Mr Hunter greeted the village seamstress cheerfully.

"Oh, Mr Hunter, I've just sent my boys to Grangeback. There have been men in here asking questions about Miss Roy. Stanley said that they looked like the same men that tried to take the girls in Chester," Miss Baker flapped.

"Was it the two men that just left?" Alex asked, already halfway out of the door.

"No, it wasn't, they left about ten minutes ago. It took me time to calm the boys down enough to send them and then those gentlemen came in asking about rooms for the tournament," Miss Baker explained.

Alex barely waited to hear what Miss Baker had to say; he wanted to get back to Grangeback to find out what was going on, but first, he needed to take Constable Cantello to talk to Miss Baker.

o-o-o

Stanley and Lee Baker arriving at Grangeback sent the already busy household into utter chaos. George immediately ordered that the girls all be barricaded in his study until he was certain it was safe.

The men of the cricket team were dispatched to search the grounds, Doctor Hales and Constable Evans were ordered to hold the door, and George organised the footmen and maids into patrols around the house.

"This is ridiculous," Grace complained as she flopped into one of the armchairs in the study.

"Not considering that there are enough muskets to arm the household twice over in the red room," Sarah replied dryly as she sat in George's chair.

"Why would a lot of muskets be more ridiculous than being locked in a study because some men were asking about Millie?" Grace frowned. Though there were social graces that had to be observed in public, in private Sarah was far happier with informality.

"Because the brigadier could have given everyone guns and sent them off on a rather dangerous hunt," Sarah replied with a shrug.

"I don't understand why we have to be locked away like this," Grace protested, "I would have accepted being confined to the house or our own rooms, but the brigadier's study?"

"What I don't understand is why there are men searching for you, Millie," Sarah said, forming a spire with her fingers and resting her chin on top of them.

Millie had been sat quietly in a corner. She hadn't protested being locked away, and she was avoiding looking at both Grace and Sarah.

"Millie?" Grace asked gently.

"I'm sorry; I can't stay here. I need to go," Millie replied, shaking her head and moving towards the door.

"Millie, whoever is trying to find you, whatever you are running from, we'll still be your friends. We can help you," Sarah urged as she tried to stop Millie from reaching the door.

"You're already in danger because of me. If I tell you anything else – there's nothing you can do to help me," Millie half sobbed. She stopped just short of the door and took a deep breath.

"Millie, who are you really?" Sarah asked softly.

"My name isn't Millie Roy. My name is Lady Mildred Serena Cowdrey-Smithe. My older sister is a powerful woman; she tried to marry me to an old Chinese man as part of her business dealings. I didn't want to get married, so I ran away," Millie explained.

"When?" Sarah asked.

"Three years ago. I was supposed to go out to India to stay with some of my sister's associates. I ran away from my escort on the dock before we had to board the ship at Southampton. Men that work for my sister have been chasing me ever since," Millie broke down and started crying. Grace rushed over and put her arms around Millie's shoulders.

"Will you still have to marry the man if your sister finds you?" Sarah asked.

"No, I don't think so. I don't know, but I do know my sister wants me dead for causing her so many problems if I don't get married on her say so," Millie cried.

"What kind of sister would do that?" Grace looked at Millie with disbelief.

"All she cares about is business. She's been that way for years. She's fifteen years older than I am. She doesn't know me at all, she was married and living on the other side of the world before I was five. I was only ever something she could use. Now I'm not useful to her anymore," Millie wailed.

"Who is your sister?" Grace asked as she moved Millie to one of the chairs opposite George's desk.

"I'd wager that her name is Lady Carol-Ann Margaret de Mandeville," Sarah sighed and shook her head. Millie stopped crying rather abruptly and turned sharply to face Sarah.

"How did you know that?" she asked, shaking slightly as she sat there. Fear was etched on every feature in Millie's face as she stared at Sarah.

Sarah didn't reply as she walked over to the door and opened it.

"Constable Evans, go find the brigadier, tell him he won't find the men in the village or around Grangeback.

Bring him and Mr Hunter back here, Miss Roy has something to tell us all," Sarah said abruptly.

The doctor looked at Sarah with a quizzical look on his face.

"You better be quick lad, no point risking our cricketers injuring themselves in an unnecessary search," Jack said to Arwyn as he stepped into the study and began to help himself to George's scotch.

Chapter 6

After Millie had told George, Alex, Jack and Arwyn her story, the brigadier had sent the girl to bed. Millie was clearly exhausted, and George needed some time to think over what he had learned.

His mind was consumed with thoughts about the chain reaction that Millie running away seemed to have set in motion. He wondered whether Sarah's parents would be dead if Millie hadn't run away from her arranged marriage.

The men had all returned, saying that there were no signs of the two men that Stanley and Lee had warned them about.

Constable Cantello had reported that there were no signs of the men in Stickleback Hollow either. Mr Hunter had breathed an inward sigh of relief when he had discovered that the men were not looking to harm Sarah.

The atmosphere at Grangeback was subdued for several days. The men practised for the tournament, and when they were not on the field, they sat and discussed tactics for their first game against Yorkshire.

"Sir Spencer used to play for Staffordshire before he was married; there is a lot of bad blood between the Staffordshire players and him over it all," Edward explained over dinner the night before their game against Yorkshire.

"And Baron Cowdrey of Tonbridge used to play for Lancashire and now plays for Staffordshire," Thomas added.

"Well, that should make for some very interesting games. Let's hope that we can use it to our advantage," George observed.

Millie had been rather silent for several days. She wasn't allowed to leave the house for fear that she would run off and neither the brigadier nor doctor thought that was a wise thing to do.

Millie was far safer at Grangeback than she was trying to run and hide from whomever Lady de Mandeville sent after her.

Everyone retired to bed early as the match was the next day. A combination of excitement and nerves meant that each of the men needed space in order to focus their minds on the task ahead of them.

Mr Hunter was the only one of the team who didn't go to his room. Instead, he made his way to the stables where the draft horses and the horses that pulled the carriages were stabled. It was also where Harald and Black Guy could be found. Harald was Alex's horse. He had been a gift from George when Sarah had first arrived. Black Guy was Sarah's horse.

With all that was going on, the grooms had been in charge of exercising the horses.

"Easy now, Harald," Alex said as the grey horse whined at the sight of his master. Mr Hunter reached up and scratched between the horse's ears.

At the sound of Alex's voice, Black Guy's head appeared over the door of his box and nudged the hunter's back.

"Starved for attention as well?" Mr Hunter chuckled as he patted the black stallion on the neck, "I know we've not been down to see you, but that won't last much longer," he soothed both creatures.

"I thought I might find you here," George's voice filtered through the night to his son.

"Is something wrong?" Alex asked, his voice not far

from being what most people would interpret as terse.

"No, my boy, I just wanted the chance to speak to you on your own. I know that I caused you a lot of pain from being selfish and prideful, but the last thing I wanted to do was to hurt you," George said gently as he walked over and fussed Black Guy.

"You've always been a selfish creature, George, when Lucy died, it got worse from all accounts. After my mother and your wife died there didn't look like there was going to be anything that would change that. Then Sarah arrived. I don't know whether it was guilt that drove you to inviting her to live here, but I do know that you've been more selfless since she came to Grangeback than at any other point in your life," Alex stared at his father with a passive expression on his face as he spoke.

"You're right, of course, but I do want you to know that I am truly sorry," George apologised.

"You know I never wanted to be the son of a gentleman. Everything about your social sphere seems so repugnant, but there is Sarah to consider," Alex said slowly.

"What are you saying?" George asked with a queer look on his face.

71

"I want you to recognise me as your son when the tournament is over. For Sarah's sake and reputation, I will be the son of a gentleman," Alex sighed.

"Does that also mean that you forgive me?" George asked with apprehension.

"It does. Things will never be what they were before, but that may not be a bad thing," Mr Hunter allowed.

"You'll keep the name of Hunter though; I wouldn't want to take that from you," George grinned broadly at his son.

"Sarah is also to remain your heir. The small amount you have left me as my entitlement is more than enough, even if I were not to marry Sarah," Alex said firmly.

"If that's what you want, then, of course, it will be so," George offered his hand to Alex. After a moment of looking at it, Mr Hunter shook it.

"I should get to bed; tomorrow will be a busy day," Alex nodded to George as he made his way back to the house. He was tempted to visit Sarah before retiring for the night, but as he looked up at her windows, he could see that the curtains were drawn and not a speck of light leaked from around them.

That's probably for the best. He thought.

o-o-o

"Out? OUT? Who chose these umpires?" the Reverend Percy Butterfield raged as he leapt out of his chair for the thirteenth time in an hour.

The scorecard read:

Yorkshire: 197 all out

Aubrey-Smith	12	c. Lumb, b. Lumb
Fleetwood-Smith	35	c. Mullaney, b. Moore
Roland-Jones	49	b. Hunter
Ingleby-Mckenzie	13	b. Hunter
Bell-Drummond	7	b. Hunter
Hamilton-Brown	24	run out (Roland-Jones)
Kohler Cadmore	28	b. Christian
Hesketh-Pritchard	4	c. Christian, b. Kitts
Douglas-Hulme	0	lbw, b. Hunter
Martin-Jenkins	17	not out
Ponsonby-Fane	8	c. Carter, b. Moore

Cheshire 98/5

Ball	34	c. Aubrey-Smith, b. Douglas Hulme
Carter	27	b. Martin-Jenkins

Blatherwick	14	c. Kohler Cadmore, b. Ponsonby-Fane
Mullaney	9	b. Hesketh-Pritchard
Hales	4	
Hutton	20	lbw, b. Ponsonby-Fane

The whole village had turned out for the game, and the teams from Staffordshire and Lancashire both watched, hoping to gain some intelligence about the teams they would play next.

There was a great deal of excitement and comments being made by the assembled crowd, but none could match those of the reverend.

"They started so well, at this rate, we'll lose this game," Reverend Butterfield said despairingly as he sat down again.

"Don't fear, reverend, they've changed bowlers again," George said cheerily. Even the prospect of Cheshire losing to Yorkshire couldn't dampen the brigadier's spirits after his late-night meeting with Mr Hunter.

"What good does that do us? Each of them already took a wicket," the reverend grumbled as he folded his arms.

Major Hesketh Vernon Hesketh-Pritchard paused before he began his run up. The whole crowd fell silent as they watched him bowl at Gordon Hales, who was not enjoying his first game as captain.

Hales kept his eye on the ball as it approached and lofted it high into the air.

"What on earth are you doing, boy?" Doctor Hales yelled as everyone watch the ball seemingly hang in the air.

Hales and Lumb had set off running, but everyone in the crowd seemed to realise what the batsmen didn't – Rory Hamilton-Brown was going to catch it.

As Hales and Lumb turned to make their second run, Hamilton-Brown closed his hands and found that the ball was not in them. Instead, it lay on the ground in front of him. In the few moments it took him to realise that he had dropped an easy catch, Hales and Lumb started to run for their third.

The crowd cheered as they made it home.

"That was lucky," Thomas laughed with relief. Neither he, Edward or Richard Hales were playing in this game, which meant that they could sit with Lady Sarah, Grace and Millie during the match.

Having the three men on hand to talk about the game and explain certain nuances made it a somewhat more enjoyable day out.

A lunch spread had been laid out for the spectators, but Cooky had filled several picnic hampers for Lady Sarah and the brigadier to take to the game for their friends and the team.

Most of the team had been too nervous to eat, so there had been enough to keep most of the Grangeback party nibbling away for the majority of the day.

"I never knew that cricket could be this much fun," Grace grinned as she clapped Lumb hitting the ball to the boundary for four.

"One of the greatest things an Englishman can do is play cricket. Another is to watch it being played in exquisite company. Since we are denied the pleasure of the former today, we are more than happy to enjoy the latter," Edward grinned.

"And what would your fiancée say about such compliments being showered on other women?" Sarah threw Edward a wry smile.

"Probably the same thing that she said last time I

tried to charm one of our rich neighbours," Edward shrugged.

"And what was that?" Sarah asked with a raised eyebrow.

"I'm going to America for two months to meet rich businessmen," Edward replied.

"It's a good thing that she is such a good sport," Thomas said, shaking his head.

"Where are Charlotte and Mary?" Sarah asked.

"Oh, they're both at St. James' Court. Neither of them particularly like cricket, so they decided to go to town until the Grand Tournament was over," Thomas replied.

"As long as they're not spending too much of our money down there, it's quite an equitable arrangement," Edward said as the stumps fell.

"You're meant to hit the ball, Gordon!" Richard shouted at his brother as the captain walked off the field.

"That's a shame, he'd just settled into the game," the brigadier sighed.

"Come on, Mr Christian, teach these northern savages how to play," the reverend shouted.

To look at the pleasant scene of the cricket affair, it

would have been easy to think that Stickleback Hollow was a serene oasis where their only concern was whether the weather would hold off until the last ball of the game.

Everyone that was watching the match between Cheshire and Yorkshire was enjoying themselves. The day finished with Cheshire winning the game with 199/7, and the trickle of people returning to their homes for the night began.

In such a crowd of people, it was easy to go unnoticed. Pattinson had been left at the house; his main duty was to guard Lady Sarah's room whether she was there or not; though he was periodically allowed out so that he could relieve himself in the garden. Had the dog been with the party from Grangeback, he could have given them some warning that they were being watched.

The warmth and joy of the day out had made even Constable Evans drop his guard so that no one, not even Mr Hunter, spotted Harry Taylor in the crowd.

Chapter 7

Cheshire's first victory was call for celebration in Stickleback Hollow. The inn was packed with villagers raising a glass to the victors. The Lancashire players were joining the revellers; some were even matching the seasoned drinkers at the inn, pint for pint.

At Grangeback, Mrs Bosworth had laid out an impressive feast for the conquering heroes, and the Reverend Percy Butterfield had brought over a crate of sherry.

It was a night of some magnificence that would not soon be forgotten – that is if any of those in attendance had been able to remember anything after the first two bottles of sherry were drunk.

When the cold light of morning crept through the windows of Grangeback, there were a lot of sore heads. The servants were up at their usual hours, though it was a considerable time later when the first of the household came down to breakfast.

It was almost lunchtime by the time everyone had risen, and Doctor Hales had come by to ensure that no one had died of alcohol poisoning in the night. Stanley and Lee Baker were also at Grangeback, bringing news that Lord Daniel Cooper was playing host to two other guests – namely Lord Joshua St. Vincent and Mr Callum St. Vincent.

The prospect of the two men being in the area as well as the men searching for Millie had put Mr Hunter in a foul temper, which was compounded by his hangover. Even Pattinson was avoiding his master as Alex sat in the corner and scowled at all and sundry who ventured too close.

Even Sarah wasn't spared his dark looks – something she was given even more of when she suggested that she go riding later that afternoon. The argument that ensued after the suggestion had to be smoothed over by the brigadier, but was sour enough to plunge the whole house into a black mood until dinner was served.

It is almost certain that the ill-feeling in the atmosphere would have continued long into the night had it not been for an unexpected visitor, who arrived just before dinner was served.

The sound of her voice echoed in the hallway of

Grangeback and could easily be heard of the muted mumblings amongst the house guests.

"What do you mean that the house is full? There are at least eight bedrooms that have never been slept in, even after the great ball of 1796!" Lady Szonja, Countess of Huntingdon, cried, as she brushed past the footmen that tried to prevent her from climbing the steps of the great house to talk to Bosworth.

"Good evening, countess, you will find them in the library," Bosworth greeted her with a slight bow.

"Thank you, Bosworth," Lady Szonja replied as she marched to the doors of the library.

"Take the countess' luggage to the clock room. I will have Mrs Bosworth prepare it at once," Bosworth instructed the footmen, and a slight smile flashed across Lady Szonja's lips.

She threw open the doors to the library and marched over to where Sarah was sat talking to Richard Hales and the Egerton brothers.

"Cousin Szonja!" Thomas and Edward chorused as they leapt to their feet. Szonja ignored both of the boys, she opened her mouth to chide Sarah, but the words choked in her throat as her eyes fell on Millie.

It had been decided that, at present, it was best to keep Millie's real identity secret from most of Stickleback Hollow. At least until after the Grand Tournament was over. There was nothing worse than a tightknit community being overzealous in defence of one of their own.

Before Lady Szonja could speak, Sarah took her by the elbow and led her to George's study. Once the door was closed, Lady Sarah waited for the countess to speak.

"You do know who that is, don't you?" Szonja demanded, looking at Sarah with wide eyes.

"Yes," Sarah replied.

"Then things are far more serious than I feared. I came to chide you for not replying to my letters. I have been sending them for three months and no response. I was beginning to fear that something terrible had happened, but this!" the countess sighed and shook her head.

"Letters?" Sarah frowned.

"Yes, letters, the twenty-four letters that I wrote to you that were left without an answering communication," Lady Szonja replied with a slight edge of irritation to her voice.

"Twenty-four? I haven't had one from you in the last three months," the crease in Sarah's brow deepened.

"That would explain the lack of response; though I find it more concerning that all twenty-four letters have failed to arrive. As things stand, I think it best if I speak to the doctor, brigadier and yourself about what I have discovered," Lady Szonja said as she sat down.

"Maybe it could wait until after dinner?" Sarah asked breezily. The countess looked at the young lady and smiled.

"Yes, it was a long journey from Huntingdon," she allowed.

The arrival of the countess had caused a shift in mood. Though Mr Hunter still refused to speak to anyone or to do more than cast about a variety of scowls, the black cloud over Grangeback had dissipated for the moment. There was only one member of the household that didn't seem all that happy that Lady Szonja was paying them a visit.

The way in which she arrived and Sarah escorting the countess out of the room had Constable Evans wondering what emergency had brought a lady like the

Countess of Huntingdon to Grangeback unannounced, especially when her own relatives seemed surprised to see her.

Chapter 8

After dinner, most of the party seemed content to go to bed early. Sarah and Constable Evans had been keen to talk to the countess after dinner, but George had insisted that everyone was to retire early; and with Mrs Bosworth's help, soon the only members of the household that were still awake were the countess and the brigadier.

"Why did you send the others to bed?" the countess asked as she sat in George's study, nursing a glass of brandy.

"I thought it best to talk to you alone first. Sarah tells me that twenty-four letters seem to have gone astray. Cause for alarm indeed, who did you send them with?" George asked as he lit his pipe and sat down opposite Lady Szonja.

"The postal office in Huntingdon," the countess replied.

"I see, then it would seem that there is an unreliable employee between the Huntingdon post office and the Stickleback Hollow postman. What was so important to tell

85

that you sent twenty-four letters?" George asked as he sipped from a glass of whisky.

"My friends in China tell me that there is trouble brewing," Lady Szonja replied.

"Is that so?" George puffed.

"Many of the officials have been concerned for some time about the increasing numbers of opium addicts and the rise of opium dens. They know that it is the East India Company that is providing the opium and turning a huge profit by doing so," the countess explained.

"But the Chinese won't allow the East India Company to trade in their country," George frowned.

"No, there are several independent businessmen and merchants that are trading with the East India Company and then transporting it into China. They are also agents for the East India Company acting within the country as well," the countess continued.

"They've been trading silk, porcelain and tea for years to us but now that the follow of silver has been reversed it is problematic?" George asked.

"From a cynical point of view, it could easily be argued that their only objection to the opium is a financial one. If you are more generous then it could be argued that it is concern for the welfare of the people that motivates their actions – but I didn't come to debate their motives, nor did I write about them," Lady Szonja replied.

"Then what was in those letters, I have my suspicions, but until you tell me, I can't know for certain," George said as he finished his whisky.

"It has long been known of Lady de Mandeville's links with the East India Company and that she is one of the principal smugglers of opium into China, but I received some other news that warranted sending on to you," the countess said, looking down at her brandy. George sighed to himself and got up to pour himself another glass of whisky.

"It must have been some discovery to need twenty-four letters to divulge it," George had a sinking feeling in his stomach.

"Some of the letters were not concerned with this matter, but more with the lack of response, I grant you, but if those letters had arrived it would have seen more suspicious," the countess said as she drained her brandy glass.

"And led to questions sooner about where the other letters were," George agreed.

"Indeed, buying time as it were. But this is a moot point a present, that is unless it becomes paramount to discover who stole the letters," the countess said as George refilled her glass.

"So what else is it that you so desperately wanted to impart?" George asked as he sat back down.

"Lady de Mandeville is not only supplying opium, but growing the poppies to produce it. Over the last few years, a great deal of her money has been invested in opium farms in India. Not only her money, but that of many of her associates that have then signed over their ownership to John Smith. There have also been rumours that upon discovering where their money was being invested, Colonel Montgomery Baird and Lady Watson-Wentworth wanted their money to be returned and their association terminated," the countess said softly.

"But Lady de Mandeville doesn't sever relationships that are profitable to her," George sighed and rubbed his forehead.

"Not only that, but they would be dangerous to her.

With the displeasure of the Chinese officials growing, the price of opium is going up. Thus the profits that Lady de Mandeville enjoys are rising. But it gets worse," the countess said.

"Worse?" George frowned.

"Though it might seem that murder in the name of profit in the opium trade is bad, orchestrating a war to increase your profits, break your opposition and solidify your control of trading in the East is worse," Lady Szonja said pointedly.

"War?" George spluttered.

"When officials start to get this displeased, war is not far away," Lady Szonja said, shaking her head.

"I see, then why is John Smith wasting so much time chasing after a pocket watch in the possession of an orphaned young lady that knows nothing of her activities? Surely she has more important things to be concerned with," George coughed as he tried to clear his throat.

"There are two difficulties. The first is that Lady de Mandeville's sister was supposed to marry one of her business contacts. As she disappeared, we both now know where she is, the wedding was called off, and now the business contact is issuing all kinds of threats to Lady de Mandeville," the countess sighed.

"You know this for a fact?" George raised an eyebrow.

"No, but the rumours circulating in certain circles are what most would accept as fact," Lady Szonja shrugged.

"And it is in these certain circles that you have come across this rumour?" George asked.

"It is. I have a contact that is trying to determine whether or not this failed match was necessitated by the actions of Colonel Montgomery Baird or whether the marriage was the cause of him stealing the watch from Lady de Mandeville, but either way, that watch is something that she now desperately needs," the countess mused.

"Do you know why the watch is so important?" the brigadier stared at his drink as he spoke.

"No, not yet, but it would be helpful to see it to determine what we can about it," the countess replied.

"I have seen it; there is nothing unusual about the watch as far as I could see," George said, shaking his head.

"If it is all the same to you, brigadier, I would like to see it," Lady Szonja insisted.

"How long are you staying at Grangeback?" George sighed.

"I will stay until the end of the Grand Tournament. I hear that Lord and Mr St. Vincent are both here, having an extra pair of eyes may be of benefit. Besides, I wish to talk to Miss Cowdrey-Smithe about her sister. She may know something about the watch or her operations that could prove useful," the countess said.

"Do you know which room Mrs Bosworth has prepared for you?" the brigadier asked.

"The clock room, I believe. Considering why I am visiting, it is something akin to irony," Lady Szonja smiled.

"Indeed." George snorted.

"Brigadier, I can't say that you seem to be too happy about my visit," Lady Szonja said lightly.

"Your company is always welcome," George said dryly.

"I see. I believe Mrs Bosworth is waiting to show me to my room, so I will bid you goodnight," the countess said coldly. She stood abruptly, placed her unfinished brandy on the table and left George to brood in his study.

Chapter 9

There was a general feeling of excitement in the village after Cheshire won their first match, especially against Yorkshire. Lancashire and Staffordshire had played each other two days after Cheshire had met Yorkshire.

Lancashire had won by a single run, and the game had proven to be an exciting one for all watching. Reverend Percy Butterfield had been especially delighted by the match and had only been too glad to offer insight into the different playing styles of both Lancashire and Staffordshire.

The two men that the reverend considered to be particularly dangerous were William Root and Mattheus Hendrik Wessels. The clergyman had ensured that he spoke to each of the team members – even those that were reserves – about the strengths and weaknesses of their styles of play and how best to neutralise them in a match situation.

Lady Sarah had listened to the different approaches

that the reverend took when discussing the players. It changed depending on the role that the player had within the team. It had proven entertaining at first, but as most of what he said was completely alien to her, it soon became dull.

The few days of relaxation with no signs of anyone approaching the manor house had improved Mr Hunter's mood enough to take Lady Sarah riding instead of attending the cricket match.

The brigadier and countess had both seemed annoyed at the apparent recklessness of the pair going riding alone, especially as Lady Szonja's only experience of the hunter was him being carried into Grangeback half-dead after being unhorsed by giant dogs. What seemed to irritate Lady Szonja even more, was that one of those giant dogs was now a member of the household and tasked with protecting Lady Sarah.

Nothing had been said by the brigadier or the countess about why she was visiting, no matter how many times Sarah asked. Constable Evans had been content to merely silently observe what was going on, but George could tell that the constable's patience was wearing thin on the matter.

Though he was aware of the growing frustration in Arwyn, he was also very aware that an argument between Sarah and Alex over an afternoon ride had plunged the household into a depression. The thought of telling anyone anything that could affect the morale of the cricket team in a negative way was something that the brigadier wasn't willing to risk until after they had played Lancashire.

Upon the advice of Reverend Percy Butterfield, there was once change made to the Cheshire side for their game against Lancashire.

Mr Richard Ball

Mr S. Carter

Mr Joseph Blatherwick

Mr Jonathan Mullaney

Mr Gordon Hales (c)

Mr James Christian (w)

Mr Luke Lumb

Mr Thomas Egerton

Mr Stuart Moore

Mr Gregory Kitts

Mr Alexander Hunter

The reserves for the team included Mr Mitchell Claydon, Mr Michael Hutton, Mr Edward Egerton, Mr Richard Hales, Mr Samuel Jones, Mr Timothy Wood and Mr Jake Walker.

At being included in the starting eleven, Thomas had been strutting around with an air of superiority which had led to his brother confiding to Sarah that Thomas was two comments away from Edward's fist connecting with his stomach.

Millie seemed to be much more relaxed whilst staying at Grangeback. Lady Sarah wasn't sure whether that was down to the close proximity of Grace or Gordon Hales.

She even seemed to be more interested in cricket than she had been before. Gordon spent most of his evenings explaining the finer points of the game to her, monopolising Millie's time and preventing the Countess of Huntingdon from speaking with her.

The hangovers that had plagued the team after their victory over Yorkshire were none existent as they took to the field. Lancashire were batting first, something that both teams seemed to be pleased about. By the break, the scorecard had Lancashire in a very commanding position.

Lancashire: 315/6

D'Oliveria	75	c. Carter, b. Hunter
Edrich	12	lbw, b. Moore
Headley	32	b. Kitts
Gunn	24	c. Hales, b. Hunter
Root	125	
Compton	27	c. Blatherwick, b. Lumb
Hardstaff	11	c. Ball, b. Egerton
Hearn	9	
Walker		
Wessels		
Mann		

The reverend had watched until D'Oliveria made his half-century, then he had simply buried his head in his hands until the innings was over. When Cheshire came out to bat, his head remained firmly set where it was.

The first few overs were the most painful to watch, though, after seven overs, things seemed to be much more settled, yet the wickets kept falling. By the time that Gordon Hales came out to bat, Cheshire were only 43/3.

Carter was still at the crease with 7 runs to his name, but he was there to act as a partner for a big scoring player, something that hadn't yet happened.

Gordon seemed to be completely composed as he went out to bat. It was clear from his composure and the way he worked with Carter that he was the only logical choice for captain.

By the time Gordon had scored 49, Carter was on 19. He settled in to bat, and Wessels fired the ball at him. The next anyone knew, Gordon was lying on the ground, screaming in agony.

At first, no one moved. Shock seemed to have hit the players and assembled crowd. The first to react was Doctor Hales. He ran onto the field, which prompted movement from both the Cheshire and Lancashire players.

Millie had burst into tears and was being comforted by Richard, who had gone a deathly shade of white.

"He'll be alright. He's not dead," Richard soothed. The significance of Richard's words were lost on Millie, Grace and Sarah, but not on Edward or Michael Hutton.

"Richard's right; could have been a lot worse," Edward said gravely.

After a few moments of the doctor examining his son, Gordon was carried off the field and taken back to the manor. Play resumed, though Wessels seemed to be far more timid in his style of play.

At the end of the 50 overs, the game was declared a draw.

Cheshire 316/6

Ball	2	b. Wessels
Carter	37	
Blatherwick	17	b. Wessels
Mullaney	17	c. Edrich, b. Mann
Hales	49	Retired due to injury
Christian	36	b. Walker
Lumb	33	c. Headley, b. Hearn
Egerton	125	

Though Reverend Percy Butterfield contended that Gordon being stretchered off shouldn't count as a wicket, most of the team were content with the draw. The journey back to Grangeback was much more sombre than it had been after their victory over Yorkshire. Most of the team was anxious to see how their captain fared, though all of them had kind things to say to Thomas for scoring so well and Carter for seeing the game through.

"How is he?" Richard asked his father as the party arrived at the house.

"He's broken his arm and dislocated his shoulder. I've done what I can for him. He needs to rest, but he has been asking for Miss Millie," the doctor smiled and showed the girl into his son's room.

"The question now is, who is going to be our captain?" Edward sighed.

"Hunter," Thomas said simply. The other players looked at him for a moment and almost all at once, began to agree what a good idea it was.

The only member of the team who seemed to disagree with them was Mr Hunter. His protests, however, were lost in the din of chatter and cheers of approval for the new captain.

Sarah watched all of this from one side. It was clear to anyone with half a brain that Mr Hunter was well regarded by most in the area, even if he liked to think that he was still little more than an outsider in the community.

Chapter 10

With two matches behind them and Gordon injured, Sunday was greeted with a rather sober attitude. Millie had slept in the chair next to Gordon's bed, and Mrs Bosworth had sent one of the maids in to help take care of the injured man.

Gordon was fortunate that he only had a dislocation and compound fracture. The process of setting the break, and putting the shoulder back into its socket, had been a painful one for the patient.

Doctor Hales was a surgeon with excellent credentials who was more than capable of setting his son's arm and putting his shoulder back where it belonged. Laudanum was given to Gordon to try and numb the pain, but even with the drug, Gordon still screamed loud enough to be heard in every corner of Grangeback.

Not only was it essential for the bone to be set quickly, but with as few people around as possible. There was nothing worse than hysteria caused by the screams of patients, and Doctor Hales was not a man to suffer hysterics in anyone.

Even though there had only been a single break, the bone had pierced the skin, and Doctor Hales was worried about infection. He had taken to checking on his son every four hours – even during the night – to ensure that he wouldn't have to amputate his arm.

As it was Sunday, the servants went to the early service that the Reverend Butterfield held. It started at 7 o'clock in the morning and meant that the servants were back at Grangeback for half-past 8 to prepare the household for services at half-past 10.

By quarter-past 10, the house was all but empty. The servants were busy going about their appointed tasks, preparing the lunch and cleaning the bedrooms. Gordon was sleeping, and Millie was sat sleeping in the chair beside him.

She had slept badly in the chair, but still refused to leave it until Gordon was stronger. Pattinson had been left to guard Gordon and Millie whilst they slept.

There had been some discussion about Constable Evans remaining behind or Mr Hunter, but the brigadier had thought that with a household full of servants, and the giant Japanese hunting dog, would be more than enough protection for the charwoman.

This all meant that the house was oddly silent. Pattinson snoozed by the fire in Gordon's room and seemed to not have a care in the world.

Outside in the grounds, the grooms were busy taking care of all the horses that had been placed in the stables during the Grand Tournament, and the gardeners and the footmen were all busy making sure that the cricket pitch was pristine. So no one was watching when three men snuck across the front lawn and peered in through the French windows of the drawing room.

Seeing that there was no one about, the three men slipped into the drawing room and silently closed the French windows behind them.

The three men checked each room in the house, careful to make sure that they weren't seen by anyone. The way that they moved would have made it clear to anyone watching that they were looking for something very specific.

When they had looked around the ground floor of

the house and not found their prize, they moved to the second floor.

They moved almost soundlessly, but the three men couldn't hide their presence from Pattinson. As the three men reached the top of the stairs, the Akita was on his feet and growling.

The sound of Pattinson growling woke Millie and Gordon.

"What's wrong with the dog?" Gordon asked groggily and then flinched as he tried to roll over on his injured arm.

"I don't know," Millie answered slowly as she got out of the chair and opened the door to the room. Pattinson pushed past Millie and bounded out into the corridor barking and growling.

The doors to the rooms that the servants were working in opened, and the hallway began to fill with people. Pattinson ignored the servants and barrelled down towards where the three interlopers had already started back down the stairs.

Pattinson was so quick that by the time the three invaders reached the bottom step of the staircase, he was barely two paces behind. The men were running out of breath by the time they reached the front door of the house.

Pattinson managed to leap and bite one of the men on the arm as they wrestled with opening the door. The man cried out in pain as Pattinson sank his teeth in and refused to let go.

After a few moments of trying to free himself from the dog, Pattinson let go, and the three men fled down the driveway.

"What is all this commotion?" Mrs Bosworth called out crossly as she came from the direction of the kitchen. When she saw Pattinson stood in the threshold of the open door, barking with blood around his mouth, her anger vanished.

"What is it, Mrs Bosworth?" Bosworth asked as he came out of the library.

"Bosworth, send one of the footmen to the church to fetch the brigadier, and send word to the constables in the village that someone broke into the house. Whoever did it will need a doctor to look at his arm," she said as she walked over to Pattinson and placed her hand on the dog's neck.

As she did this, Pattinson stopped barking and sat down.

"Good boy, Pattinson. Let's go see Cooky and get you some meat," she said warmly.

The footmen were sent immediately – one to the church and the other to the village. The brigadier was quick to leave the church with Mr Hunter and Constable Evans close behind him.

"Why is the countess here?" Alex asked as the three men made their way back toward Grangeback. It was the first time that the three of them had been alone since the Grand Tournament had begun and it was the only time that they were certain to be on their own until the tournament was over.

"Twenty-four letters are missing, and she seems to know everything including who Millie is and why she ran away," George said.

"Why does that mean she needs to stay?" Alex frowned.

"She wants to see the pocket watch and to talk to Millie," George explained.

"Why would she want to see the pocket watch?"

Arwyn asked.

"She says it's because she may be able to tell us something about the watch that we don't know," George shrugged.

"Which you don't believe?" Mr Hunter asked with a sceptical tone in his voice.

"No, I am beginning to wonder whether we can trust her. Twenty-four letters going missing is extremely strange, and she has had no desire to see the watch before now," George replied.

"Then what you are saying is that we need to keep an eye on her?" Constable Evans asked.

"I think that whilst she is here, we need to keep Millie and Sarah away from her as much as possible," the brigadier said firmly.

"I think you're right, but I will retrieve the watch," Alex sighed.

"No, not yet. Go to the pawnbrokers in Chester and see if there are any pocket watches that look similar to it. It may prove wise to have a few pocket watches on hand, especially after this latest break-in at the house," George told his son.

"Are you sure that the break-in had anything to do with the pocket watch?" Mr Hunter asked.

"No, but we are becoming more involved with a world that thrives on deceit and subterfuge. It would be wise for us to start playing our own game with them instead of merely being used as pawns or waiting for their next move," George said gruffly.

"I will look around the house and then go to the village to talk to the constables there. It would be better if this wasn't made public knowledge until after the tournament," Constable Evans said thoughtfully.

"Though that is very true, there is yet to exist a force that can stop gossip between servants or gossip in Stickleback Hollow," Mr Hunter sighed.

Chapter 11

The three men that had failed in their mission to Grangeback hid in the woods on the edge of Stickleback Hollow.

As it was still early in the year, the woods were cold and wet. The man with the injured arm had tried to bandage it up, but it was clear that he needed to get to a doctor and fast.

"We wait here until the coach to Chester comes," the man in charge hissed firmly at the other two.

"He needs a doctor. We can't wait here all day. We should start walking, then we can try and hitch a ride when someone goes past," the second uninjured man volunteered.

The first man sat and thought for a moment, before reluctantly agreeing. They started to walk towards Chester, making sure that they stayed in trees, but could see the road from where they were.

They went down into road as soon as the village of

Stickleback Hollow was out of sight. It was much easier walking on the road than it was trying to get across the fields to get to the city.

There was almost no traffic on the road as it was Sunday, but as they drew away from the village and passed farms, there were more people.

The injured arm was hidden from view, but the man looked paler with every step that he took. They had been stumbling down the road for an hour before anyone went past with a carriage or cart that could carry the three men.

The carriage that rumbled by was led by a team of four horses with sheer black coats. Their tack gleamed in the bleak spring sun and the carriage they pulled clearly belonged to someone with wealth.

The two uninjured men made a grab for the horses as they went by. They were well trained and began to slow down at the feeling of pressure on the leather.

The drive took out his whip and began to hit the two men, trying to free the horses so that they could go by. As far as the driver was concerned, anyone that tried to stop the carriage on the road was a bandit or a highwayman. Even if they were harmless travellers, it was not worth the risk to stop.

"What is it, Marsh?" a voice called out from inside the carriage.

"Three men, sir. I'm dealing with them," Mr Marsh, the driver, replied.

"No need, Marsh. Stop the coach," the voice replied.

"Very good, sir," Marsh replied. He applied the break to the carriage and gently reined the team of horses to a stop.

The three men approached the door to the carriage, as they drew closer, it was opened.

"Won't you join us, gentleman?" Lord Joshua St. Vincent leant forward as he invited the three men into the coach.

Three men looked at one another and reluctantly agreed when they heard Mr Marsh cocking a shotgun above them.

Lord St. Vincent was not alone in the coach, his brother Callum was with him.

"What is wrong with your arm?" Callum asked as the injured man climbed into the carriage.

"A dog bit me," the man replied.

"I have heard that the Akita is a rather aggressive beast. When there were three of them, they apparently did a lot of damage to Mr Hunter. That is something I would have enjoyed seeing," Lord St. Vincent said absently.

"Marsh, take us to Doctor Hamilton," Callum ordered as he closed the door. The carriage lurched forward, carrying its five occupants to the city.

"What brings you gentlemen to these parts? You're southerners by your accents," Lord St. Vincent asked.

"We are here on business," the leader of the three men replied.

"The business of kidnapping it seems," Callum yawned, and Joshua laughed slightly as the attitude of the three men changed.

"What are you talking about?" the second man asked nervously.

"Do you know who we are?" Joshua asked.

"No," the injured man replied.

"My name is Lord Joshua St. Vincent, and this is my brother, Callum St. Vincent. There is no need for you to introduce yourselves, we are well aware of whom you are. Jethro, Jessie and Jeremiah Clark. Raised as Methodists until your parents were killed and then taken to the St. Giles Workhouse in Endell Street," Joshua said coolly.

"Whilst there, the three of you discovered that you were rather adept at criminal enterprise as well as escaping from the workhouse. To begin with, you were brought back, but eventually you managed to escape and avoid those dispatched to recover you. You are currently working for a businessman known as Fitzwilliam, a Hanoverian that is living in India and has a thriving trading empire across Asia," Callum continued.

"Three years ago, Fitzwilliam was supposed to marry Lady de Mandeville's youngest sister as part of a business deal between the two of them. However, the girl disappeared, and the business deal fell apart. Since then, Fitzwilliam has been searching for the girl. In the last three years, those he has hired that have been unsuccessful. That is until word was passed to him from someone in Lady de Mandeville's organisation that she had been seen in the village of Stickleback Hollow," Lord St. Vincent leaned forward and steepled his fingers.

"That is when you were sent to Stickleback Hollow to find her. You followed her to Chester and failed to take her on the street. After such failure, you made your way to the village and have been lying in wait at her home. However, she has not been home. When you discovered that she was staying at Grangeback Manor, you waited, watching the house until you were certain that she was all but alone in there," Callum sighed and gazed out of the window.

"That was today, but you were unaware of the dog in the house or that he would be guarding her, which caused your attempt to fail," Joshua finished.

"How do you know all of that?" Jethro, the leader, asked.

"Because we work for Lady de Mandeville. With the growing unrest in China, she needs to be certain that Fitzwilliam will honour his side of the agreement if he manages to find Mildred," Callum replied with a stern expression on his face.

"And what if he chooses not to?" Jessie asked.

"Then young Jeremiah's dog bite will be the least of her health worries," Lord St. Vincent shrugged.

"You think that you can intimidate us?" Jethro laughed in disbelief.

"We don't think anything of the kind, but I would have thought that you would consider your position more carefully than that. We knew who you were, came out to find you, are taking you to see a doctor for your brother's wounds, and know everything about your lives. At no point have we shown the slightest inclination towards trepidation at being in such close quarters with you. In our job, we have dealt with individuals that have done far worse than any of you," Callum said dryly.

"So, if you would be so kind as to answer our questions, we can keep everything on a civilised level," Lord Joshua smiled.

Chapter 12

Constables Evans, McIntyre and Cantello searched the area around Grangeback and Stickleback Hollow for any signs of the three men that had broken into the house. Aside from a few patches of blood amongst the woodland, there was nothing to suggest where they had vanished to.

"It's unlikely they will come back to the house of the village now. Too many people saw them here," the countess had proclaimed when news of the men vanishing had been reported.

"That may be so, but why were they here in the first place?" George had retorted. Pattinson seemed to be the only creature near Grangeback that wasn't anxious after the invasion at the house.

He lay by the fire in the library chomping on a rather large ham bone that Cooky had rewarded the dog with.

"If we know that they are not going to try again whilst Pattinson is in the house, we should focus on the

Grand Tournament first. Once that is over, then we can worry about what those men wanted," Doctor Hales said sharply. He had been in a rather irritable state since he had operated on his son's arm and the dithering and bickering that the brigadier and countess were currently engaged in was clearly rubbing on his last nerve.

"The doctor is right," Mr Hunter agreed, "there are two matches left in the tournament. In a few days, the ball will have been held, and everything will go back to normal. Once all the visitors have gone, it will be much easier to find these three men if they are still in the area."

Both George and Szonja begrudgingly agreed to wait to discuss the matter further until the Grand Tournament was over.

Yorkshire had played Staffordshire and won. After each team had played two of their three matches the standings for the tournament were thus:

	Won	Drawn	Lost
Cheshire	1	1	0
Lancashire	1	1	0
Yorkshire	1	0	1
Staffordshire	0	0	2

With one match to play, both Lancashire and Cheshire needed to win and the other to lose in order to be named tournament champions. Yorkshire still had a chance to claim the title too, as long as both Cheshire and Lancashire lost. Staffordshire, however, was out of the running with two loses in hand.

Cheshire was to meet Staffordshire before Lancashire met Yorkshire and with Mr Hunter acting as captain, Staffordshire were clearly overconfident in their ability to beat Cheshire.

The Staffordshire team consisted of some of the most prominent personages in the northern territories:

The Honourable Frederic Ponsonby, The 6th Earl of Bessborough

The Reverend David Sheperd

Sir Pelham Warner

Sir Gabby Allen

Sir Richard Hadley

Sir Garfield St Alban Sobers

Sir Don Bradman

Lord Harris of Kent

Baron Michael Colin Cowdrey of Tonbridge

Baron Learie Nicholas Constantine

Lord Martin Bladen Hawke

Sir Tim O'Brien, 3rd Baronet of Merrion Square and Boris-in-Ossory was the only reserve they had brought for the tournament. So far, it had been a disastrous tournament for the team. Though the games had been close and well-fought, ultimately the team had lost both of the games it had played so far and beating Cheshire was their only opportunity to redeem themselves.

Mr Hunter had chosen a very different team to take the field against the Staffordshire players. His choices seemed to astound everyone, including Gordon Hales, but as captain, his decision was final and so was the outcome of the game as a result.

Mr Jake Walker

Mr Samuel Jones

Mr Mitchel Claydon

Mr Timothy Wood

Mr Richard Hales

Mr Thomas Egerton

Mr Edward Egerton

Mr James Christian (w)

Mr Stuart Moore

Mr S. Carter

Mr Alexander Hunter (c)

The reserves for the match were Mr Richard Ball, Mr Joseph Blatherwick, Mr Jonathan Mullaney, Mr Michael Hutton and Mr Luke Lumb.

The reverend had asked Mr Hunter repeatedly if he was sure that this was the team he wanted to field, and each time Alex had told him that he was certain. No one was sure why Mr Hunter had moved Carter so far down the order, except for Mr Carter, that is.

When Mr Hunter had been appointed, Carter had gone to see his new captain and asked to bat later in the line-up. Carter was a fit man, but he was ageing, and the two games he had played had left him feeling his age. Batting lower in the order meant it was unlikely that he was going to have to play for very long.

Cheshire were to bat first, and the new opening partnership walked out to a less than a warm response from the assembled crowd. After ten overs though, the crowd had changed their minds about the pair. Mr Walker and Mr Jones had managed to accumulate 75 runs between them, something that none of the other teams had accomplished so far in the tournament.

By the time their partnership was brought to an end, they had reached 150 runs. The rest of the Cheshire line up proved to be especially effective against the Staffordshire bowlers. At the end of the fifty overs, the crowd were on their feet to applaud a spectacular batting innings.

Cheshire 398/5

Walker	89	lbw, b. Lord Harris
Jones	61	c. Warner, b. Baron Cowdrey
Claydon	47	c. Hadley, b. Baron Constantine
Wood	39	c. Bradman, b. Lord Hawke
Hales, R	54	
Egerton, T.	67	b. Bradman
Egerton, E.	41	

For Staffordshire, there was no way that they could

answer such a high score, especially when their first four batsmen fell so cheaply. Before the fifty overs were done, they had achieved a respectable score, but it was not enough. For the first time in twenty years of competing in the Grand Tournament, Staffordshire had lost every game.

Staffordshire 305 all out.

Ponsonby	7	c. Jones, b. Moore
Sheperd	3	c. Christian, b. Egerton, T.
Warner	0	c. Carter, b. Egerton, T.
Allen	2	b. Egerton, T.
Hadley	59	lbw, b. Egerton, E.
Sobers	99	c. Claydon, b. Egerton, E.
Bradman	54	c. Hales, b. Hunter
Lord Harris	38	c. Moore, b. Moore
Baron Cowdrey	22	b. Egerton, E.
Baron Constantine	17	
Lord Hawke	4	b. Hunter

For Cheshire, it was the perfect close to the tournament and all that remained was to see whether Yorkshire would triumph over Lancashire or whether Lancashire and Cheshire would have to play a tie-breaker match.

Several of the villagers in Stickleback Hollow had tried to sabotage some of the Lancashire players, but they had been caught by Wilson and sent away with a lecture on sportsmanship and the threat of the innkeeper beating sportsmanship into them if they tried to sabotage them again.

There was little need to try and sabotage the team though. The match between Yorkshire and Lancashire ended in a draw and celebrations began in Stickleback Hollow.

Aside from the closing ball, the Grand Tournament was finished, and the home team had won.

Chapter 13

Vasanta Ritu is the king of seasons for the people of India. It is considered so because the weather is mild and pleasant across most of India.

It was Samit's favourite time of year as it often reminded him of his childhood spent running through the forests around his home with the children of the British Army.

They had been happy days for him, and for two months of the year, those happy memories were brought back to him in vivid daydreams.

It was also his favourite time of year because his mistress was often away from home during Vasanta Ritu. Lady de Mandeville often spent February to April in the mountains, conducting business affairs with some of her northern trade partners.

His master stayed at the house though. He was a rather pleasant man, even if he was slow-witted. It was clear to Samit that his wife had married Lord de Mandeville for his connections within society and held no affection for the man.

Lord de Mandeville seemed completely oblivious to his wife's indifference to him and only had warm and loving things to say about her and her character.

She had given him a son when they had first been married, and he was now at school in England. His existence was something of a secret, but neither he nor his father seemed to mind the arrangement.

What Samit found to be distasteful about Lady de Mandeville's treatment of her husband was the army of lovers that she paraded about under his nose that he seemed to blissfully unaware of.

Many of them were friends of the lord, though none of them seemed to have any qualms about sleeping with his wife.

Samit was certain that the annual trip that Lady de Mandeville took to Gorkha was not only a business trip but also an excuse for her to visit some lovers without being disturbed by her husband.

There were also rumours that the Gurkha War had been caused by her arrival in India in 1813, shortly before she was married to her husband. But any proof of her involvement in the war and the Treaty of Sugauli couldn't be found. Samit had spent years searching the house for evidence of the Duchess of Aumale and Montagu's complicity in the war and several conflicts since, but he had found nothing.

He had spent hours eavesdropping on conversations and heard nothing to implicate her in anything. Though he had heard plenty to worry him over the safety of Lady Sarah Montgomery Baird Watson-Wentworth.

When he received no reply to the letter he sent, he daren't send another for fear that the first had been intercepted.

Woking for Lady de Mandeville was risky at the best of times, but to be found to be spying on her for someone that she clearly considered a threat could prove deadly. If it wasn't for his master, Samit was certain that he would have left the employment for Lady de Mandeville a long time ago. For the moment, he was content to serve Lord de Mandeville and search for information that might help to free him from her and protect his childhood friend.

Chapter 14

Winter had been long and cold in Stickleback Hollow, but none had endured the hardship of it more than Mr Harry Taylor.

There were very few places to hide in a village like Stickleback Hollow, there were even fewer that a man as well-known as Harry Taylor could go unnoticed.

The Edge that rose up behind the village was riddled with natural caves, most of which were too high up for the children of the village to bother to climb to and explore.

It was in these caves that Harry had passed the winter months. He had made sure to gather some tools that could be used to help him survive during the colder months – a fishing rod and leather tools among them.

He had taken a few sheets and blankets from washing lines – something that could be attributed to the children getting carried away with games rather than a thief stalking the village.

There were wild pigs and deer in the woods that Mr

Taylor could hunt for food, made even easier by the hibernation habits of the creatures. He had been concerned at first that the caves might be home to snakes, but he hadn't seen any sign of them.

It had been a cold winter to survive, but Mr Harry Taylor was not the spoilt idiot he pretended to be. He had spent years learning how to survive in the most barren of landscapes.

When he had been in India, Lady de Mandeville had ensured that he had been taken to as many different types of terrain as she could arrange. Trading in Asia was far from standing behind a market stall in Covent Garden, and all those that Lady de Mandeville expected to work for her in the East to learn not only the art of trading but the art of survival as well.

Harry had learned the lessons well. Many of those that Lady de Mandeville sent out to learn the skills from the same social sphere as Mr Taylor never came back. Their deaths were reported as a variety of different things by newspapers from leopard attacks to bandits carrying them off when they were travelling as part of a merchant caravan.

The other essential skill that Lady de Mandeville had

her people trained in was secrecy. All-in-all, those that were trained to work for Lady de Mandeville were trained to be some of the best spies the world had to offer – or the best thieves.

It hadn't been hard for Mr Taylor to take all the items he needed to survive in the caves and it had been even easier for him to steal the letters that were due to be delivered to Grangeback from Lady Szonja.

Twenty-four letters had been intercepted all with the intention of bringing Lady Szonja to Grangeback. Harry knew that the Countess of Huntingdon would ask to see the pocket watch that Mr Taylor was waiting to retrieve.

When it was eventually produced, Mr Taylor would be on hand to take back what was stolen. In truth, it wasn't the pocket watch that was important to Lady de Mandeville, but what was inside it.

Harry didn't know what it was that was contained in the watch, but he didn't need to know in order to get it back to his employer.

With the arrival of the Grand Tournament in Stickleback Hollow, Harry had been able to come down from the cave and into the village. He could move about unseen in the crowds of people and find out what he needed to.

His time in the cave was nearly at an end, all he had to do now was wait until all the pieces fell into place.

Chapter 15

The ball to mark the end of the Grand Tournament was the highlight of the social calendar for many in Stickleback Hollow that year. Everyone was welcome at the ball, no matter what station they were born to.

The servants from Tatton Park, Grangeback and Duffleton Hall served the assembled guests food and drink before they joined the celebrations.

The gowns that Sarah, Millie and Grace wore were among some of the finest there. Mary and Charlotte had returned from St. James' Court in order to enjoy the festivities and listen to the praise being heaped on their partners.

The players of Staffordshire, Yorkshire and Lancashire were gracious in defeat as Cheshire were in victory. Children were allowed to join the festivities, though there was little in a ball to keep them entertained.

As the day turned into night, the brigadier called for

all his guests to join him on the top lawn in the gardens that ran around Grangeback.

The guests all made their way to the top field where they found a giant bonfire with four smaller fires set around it. When everyone was assembled, all five fires were lit, and four hogs were carried out on spits to be roasted over the four smaller fires to feed the guests as the evening wore on.

Barrels of ale and beer were stacked beside the hog fires and musicians began to play a variety of jigs. The more the people drank, the more enthusiastic the dancing became.

As the party wore on, the fears and cares of everyday life were forgotten, even the break-in at Grangeback seemed to be a distant memory.

Jethro and Jessie Clark moved amongst the party guests unnoticed. They danced with girls from the village until they found Grace and Millie. They danced a few jigs with the girls and then Millie wanted to return to the house to sit with Gordon.

The two men agreed to escort the two girls back to the house, but as they stepped out of the light of the bonfire and hog fires, they pulled cloths from their pockets and vials of chloroform. It took less than a minute for the cloths to be doused in the liquid and securely fixed over the mouths of the two girls.

With the amount the two girls had drunk and the strength of the two men, neither girl could struggle enough to break free. It took moments for them to fall unconscious, be picked up and carried off into the night.

No one at the celebrations had noticed the two girls leaving the ball with the two men.

On the opposite side of the estate, Mr Hunter and Lady Sarah made their way to the lodge, away from the noise and light of the ball.

"I wanted to talk to you about our relationship," Alex said as he opened the door to the lodge and held it open for Sarah.

"Oh?" Sarah asked nervously. She had a sinking feeling in her stomach.

"I spoke to my father about him recognising me as his son. We've agreed that it is for the best. You are to remain as the heir to Grangeback though. I don't want that to change," Alex explained as he shut the door behind him and went to light the lamps.

"So you're going to be Mr Alexander Webb-Kneelingroach from now on?" Sarah asked as she sat down.

"Mr Alexander Webb-Kneelingroach Hunter," Alex smiled, "it's only right that I acknowledge my mother, though it will embarrass some people."

"No longer a groundskeeper or hunter, but a gentleman. You won't know what to do with yourself," Sarah giggled.

"I have an idea or two about that," Mr Hunter replied as he came to sit beside Sarah, "I have told you many times that I would do nothing to disgrace you and I hold to that," Alex reached over and took Sarah's hands in his.

"So you are bringing an end to our relationship?" Sarah sighed and closed her eyes.

"No, the opposite. I want to spend the rest of my life watching over you, loving you, arguing with you and share the best, and worst that life has to offer with you. I want to marry you. I know that there is so much going on and until we have dealt with Lady de Mandeville and all the strange things that seem to follow you around, so I am not proposing to you now. I just wanted you to know that I love you, and I will be your husband once my father has recognised me as his son. That is if you want me to be," Mr Hunter said gently. His heart was in his throat whilst he waited for Sarah to respond.

"I do want you," Sarah grinned at the hunter. Alex laughed with relief before he took Sarah in his arms and kissed her.

"I know that we cannot spend all night here, but we have a few hours yet before we are missed," he said when they broke apart.

"Then we should make the most of it," Sarah replied.

Chapter 16

No one had noticed that Sarah and Alex had been absent from the ball for a few hours. As the festivities wore on, some of the guests passed out and had to be carried back to the village, or to the carriages that would take them back to Tatton Park or Duffleton Hall.

The Reverend Percy Butterfield had to be helped home by Stanley and Lee Baker, who came back to collect their mother an hour later.

As the bonfire burned down to embers, the number of people thinned out, and the occupants of Grangeback returned to the house.

"Has anyone seen Grace or Millie?" Sarah asked as they arrived in the entrance hall. No one had seen either of the two girls.

Mrs Bosworth bustled around the house in search of the two girls, but they were nowhere to be found.

"I'll go to Millie's house, perhaps they are there," Sarah suggested.

"I'll come with you," Constable Evans said.

"Take Harald, Arwyn, you'll both get there much faster on horseback," Alex suggested. Arwyn nodded and followed Sarah to the stable.

"Alex, join me in my study," George whispered as the rest of the household bade everyone goodnight and climbed the stairs. Doctor Hales went to visit his son and check his arm before he turned in.

"I want you to go and fetch the pocket watch tonight. I have the duplicate watches you purchased here, and I have shown one of them to the countess. She seemed content enough after she examined it, and mystified as to why John Smith would want the watch back so badly," George said as he closed the door to his study.

"What if I told you I couldn't fetch it tonight? What if it was too far away to fetch in a few hours?" Alex asked as he sat down.

"You took the watch to Scotland and hid it there?" George frowned.

"No, I thought about it, but when Heather made advances towards me, it felt a lot like a trap. I can get it tonight; I just wanted to see what you would say to that,"

Alex grinned.

"You seem awful happy tonight, my boy. Has something happened that I should know about?" George asked suspiciously.

"Nothing, father," Alex replied. At the sound of Mr Hunter addressing him as father, George paused, and an involuntary grin spread across his face.

"I see, my son, then you are merely elated after such a convincing victory?" George asked.

"Of course, father," Alex smiled back.

"Very well, can you fetch the pocket watch tonight? I want to examine it. If there is anything to be found, I think it would be best to discuss what should be done with it as soon as possible," George replied, moving the conversation back to the track it was originally on.

"I can. I'll go whilst Sarah and Arwyn are looking for Grace and Millie; it will avoid any questions about my whereabouts from them," Alex said as he got out of his chair and made for the door.

o-o-o

It didn't take Arwyn and Lady Sarah very long to reach Stickleback Hollow on Harald and Black Guy. The inn

138

was filled with noise as the Lancashire players had returned to their lodgings and continued to drink.

Wilson didn't mind as he knew that the brigadier was paying the bill, they weren't violent when they were drunk, and, eventually, they would go to bed or pass out at the table.

The streets of the village were empty as the two riders approached Millie's cottage. There was no light at the window, and it didn't look as though anyone had been to the cottage in some time.

"My lady, wait here with the horses," Constable Evans said firmly as he dismounted and handed his reins to Lady Sarah. She didn't protest as Arwyn walked towards the door of the cottage and gingerly opened it.

He wasn't inside very long as there was not much to see. Millie didn't have much in the way of possessions, and the cottage was small without many places for people to hide.

When he came back outside, he didn't need to tell Sarah that he had found nothing, the look on his face and the lack of Millie or Grace told her everything she needed to know.

"We best get back to Grangeback," Sarah said as she handed Arwyn Harald's reins.

"First we should tell Constables Cantello and McIntyre that the two girls are missing. They can launch a search and question villagers whilst we report back to the brigadier," Constable Evans said and nudged Harald in the direction of the police house.

Chapter 17

Alex moved through the forest on foot. He didn't carry a lantern as he knew every inch of the wood better than he knew the way around the village.

He walked towards the Edge. At the base of the rise, he stopped and began to dig at the foot of a birch tree. He used his hands to move the dirt. He didn't have to dig down very far until he found a small hessian sack and pulled it out of the ground.

"I wouldn't move if I were you, Hunter," Harry Taylor's voice echoed off the trees.

"Harry, I wondered when we might be seeing you again," Alex sighed as he rested his arm on his knee.

"You could have seen me whenever you liked, Hunter, I never left town," Harry replied with a nasty grin as he slowly advanced on where Alex was kneeling.

"What can I do for you, Harry?" Alex asked as pleasantly as he could.

"You can hand over the bag. But do it slowly," Harry

said as he stopped.

Alex got to his feet very slowly and turned to face his school friend. Mr Taylor held a rifle and was aiming it squarely at Alex's head. Everything in Harry's demeanour told Mr Hunter that this was not the same man that had chased him across the snow-covered fields of the boarding school.

This was a man that wouldn't hesitate to kill him if he did anything that Mr Taylor didn't like. He was still a reasonable man, but he was hardened to a point, which made him extremely dangerous.

"Put the bag on the floor and take ten steps backwards," Harry said. Mr Hunter did as he was told. He raised his hands as he moved backwards.

"Why are you doing this?" Alex asked.

"I am under orders to retrieve the property of my employer," Harry said simply as he strode forward, picked up the bag and retreated back to where he was stood before.

"Do your orders include killing me?" Alex asked.

"No, they don't. Not unless it is necessary," Harry replied.

"Is it necessary?" Mr Hunter enquired.

"Are you going to follow me?" Harry asked.

"No," Alex said.

"Then it isn't necessary for me to kill you," Mr Taylor gave Alex a wry smile as he dropped the gun barrel towards the floor.

"Why go to all this trouble for a pocket watch?" Mr Hunter asked.

"It's nothing personal, it's just business," Harry shrugged.

"But all of this, everything that happened on All Hallows' Eve -" Alex began angrily, but Harry twitching the gun made Mr Hunter check himself.

"It's an interesting thing; people that have never been involved in the business world don't seem to understand. None of it is personal. It's just business. There are things that matter on a global scale that can be torn apart by things as small as this watch. The lives of a handful of people are nothing on balance to that," Harry replied, "Now, if you will excuse me, I have an appointment to make, and I have a long way to travel."

Mr Taylor slowly melted backwards into the darkness. Alex stood and tried to listen for the sound of footsteps, but even in the relative stillness of the night, he could hear nothing.

When he was as sure as he could be that Harry was gone, Alex turned away from the edge and made his way back to Grangeback.

He arrived back to find that Sarah and Arwyn had yet to return. George was waiting for him in his study.

"Do you have the watch?" George asked as Alex shut the door.

"No, I was ambushed by Harry Taylor. He took the watch and disappeared," Mr Hunter replied.

"He did what? How could you just hand over the watch like that? We both know how important it is. Colonel Montgomery Baird gave his life to stop that watch from falling into the hands that you have given it away to," George roared. Alex sat in his chair and looked completely unmoved by the brigadier's tirade.

"The watch wasn't what was important. This is," Alex said as he took a leather cord from around his neck. At the end of the leather cord was a small silver key. He placed it carefully on George's desk.

"Where did you find this?" the brigadier asked.

"When you first gave me the pocket watch, I examined it. I found this under the mechanism. I thought it would be best to keep it separate from the watch, just in case something like this happened. I doubt that Harry knew that there was anything in the watch to look for. If this key is as important to John Smith as it seems to be, she is unlikely to tell anyone about it," Alex said.

"You're right, she can never appear weak, especially to those she employs. Do you know what it opens?" George asked.

"No, but I know that it is safer around my neck than it is anywhere else. The pocket watch has been out of her possession for a considerable length of time, the key could have been removed at any time. It will take her a while to discover where it is. That means we have some time to find out what it opens," Alex replied as he took hold of the leather cord and put it back around his neck.

"Until then, we keep it to ourselves," George said as he leant back his chair and smiled at his son.

Chapter 18

When Arwyn and Sarah returned to the house with the news that Grace and Millie were missing, it didn't take long for the household to rise from their beds.

No matter how much they had drunk, they focused very quickly with the aid of tea and the urgency that Gordon Hales' raging provided.

The injured man had risen from his bed and tried to go searching for Millie four times before his father threatened to tie him to a dining chair if he didn't calm down.

The men at the house were split into search parties, just like on All Hallows' Eve. Doctor Hales, Bosworth, Gordon Hales and the brigadier were all to remain at the house whilst Mr Hunter was in charge of the hunt. Pattinson seemed excited at the prospect of so much activity after being cooped up in the house for so long.

Mrs Bosworth brought down some of Millie and Grace's clothes to help Pattinson pick up their scent. Before the search parties set out, the Lancashire team, in the company of Constable Cantello and Constable Evans arrived at Grangeback to help with the search.

It took another hour to re-organise the search parties, but when they were ready, they agreed to search for two hours and report back to the house.

The brigadier tried to send the ladies of the house back to bed as the men departed, but no one was in the right frame of mind to sleep.

Lady Sarah sat with Gordon Hales in the library, the brigadier talked with the doctor, and countess in his study and the rest of the household busied themselves in the kitchen, preparing food and hot drinks for when the men returned.

"I'm beginning to think that we should avoid having balls in the future," Sarah said as Gordon tapped his fingers with agitation on the arms of the high-backed leather chair he was sat in.

"Why is that?" Gordon asked with a distracted air.

"Because every time we hold a ball, someone goes missing and then we are up half the night looking for them," Sarah replied. Gordon laughed in spite of himself,

"That is true, but none disappeared from a ball before you arrived in the county."

"Well then, it's decided. For the sake of public safety, I shall never again attend a ball," Sarah said in a resolute manner. Gordon laughed harder and felt some of the weight of worry lift from his shoulders.

"Thank you for that," Gordon said when he managed to catch his breath.

"You're welcome. They will find her. You needn't worry," Sarah soothed.

"I don't think I have ever felt this way about a woman before. I can't stop thinking about her. When I am away from her, I just want to be around her. The idea that she is gone and I will never see her again physically hurts," Gordon sighed.

"I know how you feel." a smile curled the corner of Sarah's mouth as she spoke.

"Hunter?" Gordon asked, and Sarah nodded, "He's a good man. He deserves a good woman. Does he feel the same way?"

"Does Millie?" Sarah asked.

"She does."

"He does."

The pair lapsed into silence.

"Millie, she told me she isn't really a charwoman. Is it true?" Gordon broke the silence after half an hour.

"Would it matter if she were?" Sarah asked.

"No, I love her. I would love her no matter who she was or what she did," Gordon said defensively.

"She needs that more than most," Sarah smiled.

"You know who she really is?" Gordon asked.

"Her name is Millie; the rest is up to her to tell you. But it is nothing if you really love her," Sarah replied.

After two hours, the search parties returned without having found any sign of Grace or Millie. They set again to search for another three hours and came back again with nothing.

After they had been out and searched for four hours, Mr Hunter came back to Grangeback with two unexpected guests in tow.

Chapter 19

Mr Hunter had led his party back past the lodge on their final search. The men were cold and hungry, but Pattinson was asleep on his feet.

The hunter knew that they wouldn't be going out to search again for a few hours, so he took the dog home to rest.

When he opened the door to the lodge, he found Lord Joshua St. Vincent and Mr Callum St. Vincent were waiting for him. Even in his fatigued state, Pattinson was immediately on his guard.

"Calm your attack dog down, we're not here to harm you or yours," Joshua said with a wave of his hand.

"What makes you think I won't harm you for what you did to Sarah?" Mr Hunter demanded as he struggled to keep his own anger checked.

"That wasn't personal. It was just business," Joshua shrugged.

"Much like what happened to those three women?"

Alex shouted.

"There are consequences to failure in our business. They knew the cost of failure and the reward for success," Callum replied.

"Why are you here?" Alex ignored Callum's response.

"We have some information that you will find useful in discovering where young Mildred and Grace are," Joshua said as he got to his feet and placed his top hat on his head.

"Why would you help find them?" Mr Hunter frowned.

"It's business," Joshua smiled. He refused to say anything further and with no other leads to the whereabouts of the two girls; he had no choice but to agree to work with the two men.

After Alex had fed Pattinson and put him to bed, he set off for Grangeback with his search party and the two unexpected guests.

When they arrived at the manor house, the brigadier and countess gave the two St. Vincents the same greeting that Mr Hunter had. After Alex had explained the situation, George dismissed the search parties and took Joshua,

Callum, Alex, Arwyn, Szonja and Jack to the library where Sarah and Gordon were still sat.

"You!" Sarah cried as Lord St. Vincent swaggered into the room.

"They know where Millie and Grace are," Alex told her.

"At the asylum perhaps? You do have a habit of imprisoning women there," Sarah scowled at the two men.

"You were there for your own safety; you were not treated badly during your time there, and besides. It was just business," Joshua said smarmily.

"If I hear that one more time, I am going to let Pattinson rip your throat out," Alex growled.

"You want to discuss the matter at hand then, very well. My brother has all the relevant details," Lord St. Vincent said as he sat down.

"Three men attempted to abduct the two ladies from the city of Chester a few weeks ago. Their names were Jethro Clark, Jessie Clark and Jeremiah Clark. Brothers with an unhappy history but found their particular skill set was valuable to a man known as Fitzwilliam. For many years Fitzwilliam has been the main competition for our employer; however, in the last five years, it became apparent that with the shifting Asian markets, an alliance would benefit them both," Callum began.

"Traditionalists at heart, they felt the best way to seal their association was through marriage, though it had to wait two years until my employer's sister became of age. The whole scheme was kept from her until she was old enough to marry. When she discovered the arranged marriage, she fled. You know her as Millie, though her real name is Lady Mildred Serena Cowdrey-Smithe," Joshua continued.

"The moment she fled, Fitzwilliam sent the Clark brothers out in search of her. Due to the indiscretion of a member of our organisation, Fitzwilliam was made aware of her location, and the Clark brothers came to Cheshire to acquire her. Not only was Fitzwilliam told of Millie, but also of Miss Read, but we shall come to that in a moment," Callum said.

"When our employer learned of the situation, we were dispatched to discover whether Fitzwilliam's searching meant he wished to honour the business deal, or if he was merely looking for Millie to use her as a bargaining chip. The Clark brothers proved to be almost useless in providing us with the information we required, but Jeremiah, who was injured by the dog, let slip that they had been sent for Millie and Grace. Rather than dispatch the three gentlemen, we thought it best to observe what action they took," Joshua stood up and began to pace the room.

"Though we haven't had the confirmation we required, it seems that Fitzwilliam intends to indulge one of the Middle Eastern customs of multiple wives that he can use as hostages in business dealings," Callum finished.

"You want our help in retrieving the two girls so that you can use them in the same way?" the doctor laughed in disbelief.

"Not precisely, but it is true that we are unable to acquire them on our own," Joshua allowed.

"Then what is it you are expecting?" Sarah demanded.

"We help each other. We retrieve the two girls. Mildred comes back to our employer with us, and Grace comes back to Grangeback," Callum smiled.

"You will need to talk over what you consider the best course of action; we will be waiting at the inn for your decision. But if you are not there within the hour, we will go to retrieve Mildred on our own," Joshua said, motioning to his brother. The two men nodded to their reluctant hosts and left.

Chapter 20

"You can't work with those men!" Gordon said desperately. The St. Vincent brothers were barely out of the room when Master Hales exploded.

"Though they are men that we cannot trust, as long as our goals remain the same, they aren't going to betray us. If we make a deal with them, they won't break it," the countess said as she looked over the faces of everyone in the room.

"I don't understand what is going on, but you can't let them take Millie," Gordon slammed his good fist down on the arm of his chair.

"Doctor Hales, can you find out if any doctors in Chester or the villages between here and the city saw Jeremiah Clark and the dog bite on his arm?" Sarah asked slowly.

"I can, it will take some time. If I could have the assistance of Constables Evans, McIntyre and Cantello, it would be a much faster process," Jack said with a bemused expression on his face.

"What are you thinking?" Alex asked.

"We can't let the St. Vincent brothers take Millie back to Lady de Mandeville, but we need their help in finding where Grace and Millie are. As long as they know the location but need our muscle, we are at a disadvantage," Sarah explained.

"But if we can find the brothers by following the trial from the doctor, then we won't need the St. Vincent brothers anymore," Alex finished her thought.

"Exactly. Lord St. Vincent will want Mr Hunter and Constable Evans to help him. If the rest of us can go to the doctors and find out what we can about the Clark brothers, then we have a chance of saving Millie and Grace. We can use the police house in Chester to leave messages so that the St. Vincent brothers won't know what we have discovered," Sarah smiled.

"It is a good plan. It is our best chance of retrieving the two girls," the brigadier agreed.

"Then we'll go to meet with Joshua and Callum and check-in at the police house in twelve hours," Alex said, looking at Arwyn, who nodded his agreement.

A knock at the door brought an end to the discussion in the library.v

"Enter," the brigadier said.

"A telegram has arrived for the countess, sir. It is marked urgent," Bosworth said as he walked into the room carrying a message on a silver platter.

"Thank you, Bosworth," the countess said as she picked up the message and read through the contents of it.

"The machinations of business may have to wait," the countess said slowly.

"What do you mean?" George frowned and the countess held out the telegram to the brigadier.

"What does it say?" Doctor Hales asked.

"URGENT STOP CHINESE DECLARED WAR STOP OPIUM SEIZED STOP ALL AGENTS RECALLED STOP ALL SAILING SUSPENDED STOP," George read the telegram.

"What does that mean?" Mr Hunter frowned.

"It means that the countess and I will be away for a while and Lord and Mr St. Vincent will both be otherwise engaged. Millie and Grace won't be leaving the country though, so they will be safe enough for the moment,"

George explained.

"What is going on?" Gordon asked.

"We are at war with China over the opium trade. There will be no ships sailing aside from those that the military allow. No one will be allowed to leave the country that isn't sailing on the business of the government or its subsidiaries," the countess explained.

"Then where will the four of you be?" Sarah frowned.

"We will be going to China. We have work to do," George replied as he strode over and threw the note on the fire.

"Come, they will be waiting for us," the countess said.

"Until we return, don't do anything foolish," George smiled as he hugged his son and ward, shook hands with Jack, Arwyn and Gordon, "look after them, Bosworth."

"Yes, sir," Bosworth bowed slightly as the pair left the room, and the door to the library was closed.

"Well, what do we do now?" Arwyn asked

~*~*~

Need to know what happens yet? The next book in the series is waiting for you now!

The bodies are piling up in Stickleback Hollow, and her ladyship's the prime suspect! Can she clear her name before the killer strikes again?

Tinker, Tailor, Soldier, Die, Book 6 in the Mysteries of Stickleback Hollow is waiting for you now.

~*~*~

Looking for more than just books? You can get the latest releases from me, signed paperbacks and hardbacks, mugs, t-shirts, journals and much more from my Read Round the Clock Shopify store.

~*~*~

Love **A Bonfire Surprise in Stickleback Hollow**? Then go back to beginning and see where it all started in **A Thief in Stickleback Hollow**.

Her arrival in England has exposed a mysterious conspiracy. Her parents deaths are tied to it, but will investigating it lead to her own death?

~*~*~

Want to help a reader out? Review are crucial when it comes to helping readers choose their next book and you can help them by leaving just a few sentences about this book as a review. It doesn't have to be anything fancy, just what you liked about the book and who you think might like to read it.

If you don't have time to leave a review or don't feel confident writing one, recommending a book to your family, friends and co-workers can help them choose their next book, so feel free to spread the word.

Historical Note

Each of the cricketers for the Staffordshire, Lancashire and Yorkshire sides in this book are named after real cricketers (some living, some dead), of course, the majority of characters in the books do have the combined names of cricketers too; however, each of the teams had a theme that had to be adhered to in order to include the cricketers in this particular book.

The Cheshire team is mostly formed of characters that have been named after one or more of the Nottinghamshire County Cricketers (my club - #outlawsforever). The Yorkshire team has been formed of players that all have double-barrelled surnames (my favourite being Kohler Cadmore for how it rolls off the tongue); the Staffordshire team has been formed of players that all had some form of title and the Lancashire team has been formed of cricketing families.

The more astute amongst you may notice that Billy Root of Nottinghamshire is playing for Lancashire rather than Cheshire, along with Riki Wessels. This is because I have chosen my favourite cricketers (based on their style of play) out of the families. Not only this, but it gave me the chance to have the Cheshire players comment on how much they weren't looking forward to playing against a team with an outfield that could actually play.

This is a rewritten account of a conversation that I was privy to at the 2017 T20 Finals Day when the Notts Outlaws beat the Birmingham Bears to the title. Two young gentlemen sat beside me, and Birmingham supporters, after watching Billy Root move like greased lightning (one of the reasons I feel he is most deserving of the nickname, Rocketman Root) commented, "It's not fair; you have a team that can actually field." This conversation then turned to discussing the speed with which Billy Root can move and how when batting, most of his partners often struggle to not be overtaken. (For those of you that can remember how frighteningly fast James Taylor was running between wickets, just imagine how incredible it would have been to watch Billy Root and James Taylor batting together and running sixes when most people could only manage threes)

Though there are several blogs that detail for whom each character is named in these books, I would like to throw in a special mention (and not at all a historical note) to the character of Harry Taylor. Named for Harry Gurney and James Taylor, his reputation as a legendary batsman in this book is something of a double nod to the two players. Taylor was a legendary batsman before he was forced to retire from the game and Harry is a true number 11, who I expect will turn around and shock us all with his first century any day now.* He is also a villain because it is pretty much as far from the truth about the character of either of his namesakes as you can get.

Polio (Poliomyelitis or infantile paralysis) was rampant during the 1800s, causing deaths and deformities. It wasn't until the introduction of a vaccine in 1955 that the disease began to decline and in many western countries, it has been decades since the last diagnosed case. There are three different types of polio, but all three cause some form of paralysis or deformity. Besides polio, there was also the risk of post-polio syndrome that affected those that had survived polio anywhere from ten to forty years after they have recovered from the initial infection. PPS is the continued weakening of muscles that polio infected, increased levels of fatigue, joint pain, bone deformities and muscle deterioration. There isn't any known cause of post-polio syndrome or an effective treatment for it.

The workhouses in Chester in 1839 were run by an incorporation of the parishes of the Holy Trinity, St Bridget, St John the Baptist, St Martin, St Mary on the Hill, St Michael, St Olave, St Oswald and St Peter. The incorporation was formed in 1762. There were several different poor houses, but the most prominent seems to have been the Roodee workhouse.

It was used for spinning cotton, and in 1767 a fire broke out that killed sixty children, twelve men and five women. Despite this disaster, the workhouses in Chester had an excellent reputation. Due to the incorporation status of the parishes of Chester, the city was exempt from the changes that were made in 1834 to the 1815 Poor Law, meaning that they could still effectively look after the needs of the poor. In 1831 Hemmingway (who you may remember toured the Cheshire Lunatic Asylum) also had high praise for the Roodee workhouse.

"There are few places in the kingdom where the comforts of the poor are so efficiently provided for, as in this institution. The board of guardians meet every Thursday, when each individual case of the out-poor is brought before them; and when each inmate of the house is at liberty to state his complaint, if he have any to prefer. The internal management is truly excellent, and exhibits an example that may be advantageously nutritious; their treatment, gentle and humane, while an appearance of cleanliness and an air of comparative comfort are prominently discoverable through the whole of the little community."

Workhouses were not pleasant places on the whole (*as Oliver Twist shows*) but they were often the only places that children and poor people could go to live when they had nowhere else to go. Often it was because they were too poor, old or ill to look after themselves. Unmarried pregnant women that their families had disowned also ended up in the workhouse in order to give birth. Poor children, whether in a workhouse or not, had a very high mortality rate during the early 1800s. In Sheffield, for example, between 1837 and 1841 of the 11,944 deaths in the Sheffield General Infirmary, more than half of them were children under five. 2,983 were children that didn't survive their first year, 1,511 were aged just 1 year old, and 1,544 were between the ages of 2 and 4.

Gun laws didn't really exist in Great Britain until the 1920 Firearms Act, so it may have been unusual for a gun to be discharged on the streets of Chester, but it wasn't impossible. Lady Sarah would have been well within her rights to not only own a pistol but to carry it with her at all times.

Humbugs as items of confectionary existed as early as 1820 though they were originally created not as a treat but as a throat lozenge.

Harry Ogden was a man from Lancashire that is credited with opening the first bookmakers in the 1790s in London.

The Great Wen is a nickname for London that was coined by William Cobbett in the 1820s. Cobbett was a champion of rural England, and the people of Stickleback Hollow would certainly have been aware of his pamphlets that Cobbett thought of as a pathological swelling on the face of the nation.

As Grangeback is a fictional place, there was no ball held in 1796 – great or otherwise. However, there are a number of charity balls that have been held across Cheshire for a considerable period of time. In 1824 a charity ball in Chester raised over £500, the equivalent of £20,960 today.

Though there are instances of items disappearing in the post in the United Kingdom, the Royal Mail postal service is still a rather reliable service. For twenty-four letters to go astray is more than a little suspicious. Interestingly, the postal service in the United Kingdom was established back in 1516 when Henry VII created the position of "Master of the

Posts" which later evolved into the office of Postmaster General.

This service was not available to the public until 1635 when Charles I made the service available to all. But rather than paying to post an item, people paid to receive them. At this point there were several different providers of postal service; that is until 1654 when Oliver Cromwell created a monopoly in the form of the Office of Postage. But this only applied to England.

Charges for post varied until 1657 when fixed postal rates were brought in and in 1660, Charles II established the General Post Office. The year after, the first postage stamp was used, and the first Postmaster General was appointed.

During the 1700s mail coaches were introduced, first between Bristol and London. It wasn't until 1793 that uniformed postmen were first seen on the streets either. In 1830 the first mail train ran between Liverpool and Manchester. Then came Rowland Hill in 1837, he created the first adhesive postage stamp and was later knighted for it.

This stamp became the Penny Black in 1840, but before this, the Post Office Money order system was established in 1838.

There were a great many changes that occurred between 1840 and the present day for Royal Mail; however, those I shall save for another time when the people of Stickleback Hollow reach those landmarks.

The first opium war between China and the British East India Company began in 1839 on 18th March and lasted for 3 years, 5 months, 1 week and 4 days. It was during this war that Hong Kong Island became part of the British territories. The British won the war. The war began because China was largely self-sufficient at the time and though traded tea and silks with the Western world, there was virtually no exportation from the west into China.

The East India Company began to auction opium that had been grown on large plantations in India to independent foreign traders who then sold it to traders on the Chinese coast, who took the opium into the Chinese interior. This reversed the flow of European silver and created a large number of opium addicts in China that alarmed officials. The Daoguang Emperor rejected proposals to legalise and tax opium in 1839 and tried to solve the problem by abolishing the trade and appointing Viceroy Lin Zexu.

It is during this war that the British used its gunnery and naval power to ensure the defeat of the Chinese and led to the coining of the phrase, gunboat diplomacy. But more shall be said about what happened in the Opium Wars in the next book.

Papaver somniferum is the Latin name for the poppies that poppy seeds, poppy seed oil and opium both come from. The seed pods from this particular poppy were used to create tinctures such as laudanum and other opiates. The pods are cut, and the latex that comes from the green seed pods is allowed to dry before it is collected. This is where we get opium from (not the seeds themselves as many people think).

When it comes to records in cricket, especially one day

cricket, most cricket fans will know that it is entirely possible to achieve over 125 runs in a one day game. There is one man who holds a multitude of records in the one day arena which include the highest score of an English batsman in a One Day International and the highest score in a domestic One Day competition – Alex Hales.

I am pleased to say that I was at Trent Bridge witnessing the ten records that were set on the day that Hales achieved the highest score of an English batsman in an ODI and I was also at lord's to witness not only Nottinghamshire winning the One Day trophy (in what was a most sensational season for the team) but Hales achieving the highest domestic One Day score as well as a few other records. That I was wearing the same outfit on both occasions clearly had no bearing on the outcome. On a completely unrelated note, it is a strange quirk of the English language that "a" should apply to the long hand of One Day International and "an" should apply to ODI.

Cricket was and still is an extremely dangerous sport to play. The comments of Richard Hales over his brother not being dead may seem to be in poor taste and rather flippant to readers unacquainted with the sport, but those who are cricket fans will be all too aware of those who have died during cricket matches or as a result of the injuries that they received whilst playing.

One of the first recorded deaths playing cricket was on 28th August 1624 when Jasper Vinall was struck on the head by a bat. On 29th June 1870, George Summers died having been struck on the head by a cricket ball four days earlier. On 17th January 1959, Abdul Aziz was struck over the heart by a cricket ball and died. On 20th February 1998 Raman Lamba was struck on the head by a cricket ball whilst fielding and died. Darryn Randall was killed on 27th October 2013 when he was struck on the head by a ball, and on 27th November 2014, Phillip Hughes was struck on the neck by a cricket ball and died.

These are just a few deaths that have occurred in the sport, which is to say nothing of the injuries. After Phillip Hughes' death, there were changes made to include neck protectors with batting helmets. However, bowlers and most fielders still play without helmets. Though this may seem to be of little consequence, earlier this year (2017) Luke Fletcher of Nottinghamshire County Cricket Club was bowling and had the ball deflected back at his head from a very short distance. It was an accident, and in most cases, bowlers have time to duck under such shots. On this occasion though, it was an almost instantaneous event.

Luckily the Bulwell Bomber (as he is affectionately known) sat up after the event and even managed to walk off the field. He was taken to the hospital and given the rest of the season off, but it was miraculous that his injuries were not more severe given what transpired. (I will admit I was in tears when it happened – and I wasn't the only one)

When it came to broken bones, there is a history of professionals being involved in setting them. Traction was used to set bones as far back as the 16th century. In the 1700s, there were people called bone setters rather than doctors that were responsible for setting broken bones. Sarah Mapp was one of the most famous bone setters at that time. Bone setters were renowned for their nimble fingers and very well respected amongst the people.

By the time the Victorian age began, there were changes in the air that meant that doctors had to be registered to practice medicine, and it was surgeons that set broken bones rather than bone setters. The bone setter profession still persisted, but it was the poor that went to bone setters for help as they were cheaper than doctors.

Single breaks were known as compound fractures and were simple to set. Arms were easier to set than broken legs due to the muscles, and dislocations were the easiest bone injuries to correct. Multiple breaks of a bone still presented a difficulty to even the most competent of surgeons. Though they were possible to set, if infection set into the affected limb, it had to be amputated.

Amputation prevented blood poisoning or sepsis from setting in and was the only alternative to death in these cases as antibiotics had yet to be invented.

There is one point that some cricket fans may have noticed

that I have chosen to omit from this story, and that is the inclusion of extras during the cricket matches. The reason for this is purely that within the confines of a story, there isn't the space to teach every one of the cricket laws and include things such as extras. Those particulars shall be left for the *Companion Guide to Stickleback Hollow*.

The Gurkha War is also known as the Anglo-Nepalese War and took place between 1814 and 1816. It came about because of border disputes between the East India Company, Garhwal Kingdom, Patiala State, Kingdom of Sikkim and the Kingdom of Gorkha. The war ended with the signing of the Treaty of Sugauli. It was a British victory, but the Nepalese maintained their independence from the British. However, they did lose one-third of their territory to Britain.

The St. Giles Workhouse in Endell Street was opened in 1725, and by 1777 it could hold 520 inmates. In 1844, ten years after the 1834 Poor Law Amendment Act, the workhouse had an infirmary added to the north side of Vinegar Lane. The site included a men's yard, a women's yard, the workhouse, baths and wash houses, the infirmary, a drying yard and a stone yard. In 1865 the workhouse was the subject of several articles that revealed the terrible condition of the buildings. The articles provoked a public outcry that led to the Metropolitan Poor Act in 1867, which resulted in the creation of the Metropolitan Asylums Board. In 1914 the workhouse became part of the Holborn Poor Law Union. Since then all the former workhouse buildings have been demolished.

Wild bears have been extinct in the British Isles since around 1000 AD, so when Harry Taylor was hiding in the caves around Stickleback Hollow, he was in no danger of coming across one. The wild pigs mentioned in the story are not wild boars. They are pigs that escaped from the farms and eventually created their own wild population in the woods.

Wild Boars have been extinct in the UK since around 1400 AD. Boars were becoming rare in 1087, so William the Conqueror created the forestry law that punished people for unlawfully killing a boar. Charles I attempted to reintroduce wild boars to the New Forest, but this proved to be unsuccessful due to the Civil War that not only claimed his life, but exterminated the wild boar population. In 1980 wild boars were being farmed in the UK. By the 1990s several had escaped and re-established themselves in Kent, Dorset, Dartmoor and the Forest of Dean. It is also reported that some of the wild boar have made their way to Monmouthshire in Wales.

Chloroform was discovered in 1830 by a German pharmacist called Moldenhawer. He wasn't the only one to create it though, in 1831 Samuel Guthrie, an American doctor also created chloroform. However, it wasn't until 1834 that Jean-Batiste Dumas determined the formula for chloroform and named it. It wasn't until the 1850s that chloroform was commercially produced or the properties of the drug were known. Though there were other drugs that I could have chosen to knock out Grace and Millie, it seemed fitting that something newly discovered and potent would be at the disposal of businesspeople as powerful as Fitzwilliam and Lady de Mandeville.

*Before this book was sent to printing, Harry Gurney made a career-best batting score of 42 in the final match of the County Championship 2017 Division 2 between Sussex and Nottinghamshire. Something that many Nottinghamshire supporters still can't quite believe.

About the Series

Mysteries abound

When her parents die from fever, Lady Sarah Montgomery Baird Watson-Wentworth has to leave India, a land she was born and raised in, and travel to England for the first time. Finding it almost impossible to adjust to London society, Sarah flees to the county of Cheshire and the country estate of Grangeback that borders the village of Stickleback Hollow. A place filled with oddballs, eccentrics and more suspicious characters than you can shake a stick at, Sarah feels more at home in the sleepy little village than she ever did in the big city, however, even sleepy little villages have mysteries that must be solved.

Set in Victorian England, the Mysteries of Stickleback Hollow follows the crime solving efforts of Constable Arwyn Evans, Mr. Alexander Hunter and Lady Sarah Montgomery Baird Watson-Wentworth. From theft to murder, supernatural occurrences and missing people, Stickleback Hollow is a

magical place filled with oddballs, outcasts, rogues, eccentrics and ragamuffins.

Preview from the next book

Tinker, Tailor, Soldier, Die

When Mr Hunter returned to Stickleback that evening, Edryd and Derwyn were waiting with Doctor Hales to dine with him. The dinner was a silent, and stilted affair shrouded in the foul mood that seeing Sarah in prison had sunk Alex into.

The moment that he was finished eating, he rose from the table and went to lock himself in his father's study.

Nothing about the situation made any sense to him. There was no one that wanted to see Lady Sarah dead, not even Lady de Mandeville, and yet someone had made it his business to frame her for murder.

He spent the whole night sat in the brigadier's study, his mind picking over everything that Arwyn had told him, everything the coroner had told him and everything that Lady Sarah had said.

He had spent so long lost in his thoughts that he didn't realise that the night had ended. He didn't hear Mrs Bosworth knock at the study door and he didn't hear her unlock the door from the outside.

"Mr Hunter, Constable Evans and Miss Wessex are here. You best come," Mrs Bosworth gently told him as she roused him from his musings and Pattison padded into the room and placed his head in Alex's lap.

Alex sighed, roughly stroked his Japanese hunting dog, and then stood to follow Mrs Bosworth to the drawing room where Miss Wessex and Arwyn were waiting.

The rest of the household had yet to rise, save for the servants, so it was an odd hour for anyone to be calling, yet the time of day didn't enter into Mr Hunter's thinking until he saw the bloodshot eyes of Elizabeth Wessex that told of desperate weeping.

"What's happened?" Alex frowned as he looked between the pair.

"Lord Cooper is missing," Arwyn said quietly.

"Mrs Bosworth, please take care of Miss Wessex. The

constable and I are going to find our wayward neighbour," Alex sighed.

Miss Wessex made to open her mouth to thank the hunter, but instead of thanks, another flood of tears burst forth.

Alex saddled Black Guy and Harald for Arwyn and him to ride, and the pair set off for Duffleton Hall with Pattison trotting along beside them.

The Akita had spent far too long cooped up inside the house, and now that he was out, he raced off in all directions before he came back to try and tangle himself in the legs of Harald.

Both the constable and hunter were relieved when they reached Duffleton Hall and could leave the dog outside to race around the grounds.

The butler at Duffleton informed the two men that Lord Daniel Cooper hadn't been seen at the house for several days, but that he had been going to see his mother at Tatton Park.

The road between Stickleback Hollow and Tatton Park was a good road, though it was still the afternoon by the time Arwyn and Alex arrived at the great house belonging to the Egerton family.

Mrs Ruth Cooper was hardly pleased to see the two men and sent them away saying,

"I haven't seen my son since he took up with the Wessex harlot."

There was nothing else that she would say to the men. By the time the constable and the hunter returned to Stickleback Hollow, the afternoon was fading fast, and neither man had eaten all day. They stopped at Wilson's Inn to eat.

"Do you think that Lord Cooper being missing is down to the Nursery Killer?" Arwyn asked in a low voice. Though they were surrounded by people that didn't believe that Lady Sarah could possibly have committed the murders, there were a lot of strangers in the village that seemed to be listening to every conversation with earnest interest.

"I don't know. You should go back to Duffleton and find out the date that Daniel left for Tatton Park. If he is dead and the Nursery Killer is responsible, then it will be enough to free Sarah – as long as she was already in prison when he vanished," Alex hissed as he let his eyes scan over the people sat in the inn to ensure that no one was listening to them.

"What are you going to do?" Arwyn asked as he drained the last of the ale from the mug in front of him.

"I am going to take Pattinson to search the woods. Daniel was going to Tatton Park, so I will search off the road and see if I can find any signs of where he might have gone," Alex replied.

"I will meet you at the police house later tonight, and I will tell you what I've found," Arwyn said as he stood up to leave.

"Are you going to spend any time talking to your brother and father at all?" Alex asked with an amused expression as Constable Evans made to turn away from him.

"You're a fine one to talk about estranged fathers," Arwyn said as he shot the hunter a dirty look over his shoulder.

"I made my peace with my father, yours came all this way, and he's still here. I don't think he's come just to see Doctor Hales or to keep Lady Sarah company," Alex shrugged in reply.

"Shouldn't you be doing something else?" Arwyn sighed.

"Think about it, my friend," Mr Hunter laughed as he watched Arwyn walk out of the inn, shaking his head.

Alex waited in Wilson's Inn for half an hour before he left. He made sure that he had taken a mental note of all those in the inn that seemed to be paying too much attention to the drinks in front of them.

In his experience, those that focused their eyes on their drinks in a bar, especially when in a group, were those who were going to cause the most trouble. Their eyes were trained on a single spot so that their ears could focus on something else.

Pattinson had been sleeping whilst the two men ate, but now that Mr Hunter was on his feet again, the dog was only too happy to follow him.

Alex left Harald and Black Guy at the inn and made his way through the village and forests on foot. When he was done with his search and had spoken to Arwyn, he would lead the two horses back to Grangeback. But until then, the creatures had done enough for one day.

He made his way up through the trees, making sure

that he doubled back to confuse anyone that might be following them.

Pattinson had his nose in the air and was on alert as everything in the way that Mr Hunter moved told the dog that they were hunting something.

When Alex was certain that they weren't being followed, he made his way to the road that led through the woods from Duffleton Hall.

The trees were the best place for the hunter to start his search as between the woods and Duffleton Hall there was nothing but open land and farms that would have seen anyone that attacked the young lord on the road.

In the woods, there were places for bandits, highwaymen and vagrants to hide, and though Alex did his best to ensure that the forests were free from danger, he had been away, and a wanderer on the road was as much of a threat to an unsuspecting rider as a gang that used the trees as their hunting grounds.

The light was bleeding from the sky as the hunter and the hunting dog reached the base of the Edge that rose out of the trees and cast a shadow across the village.

The Edge was a strange place that many people

believe held strong magic, but to Alex, it was merely the site where he had saved Lady Sarah from three women and gained a hunting dog in the process.

The hunter had seen several signs that people had passed through the woods, but the trail he now followed was one that left him with an unsettled feeling in his stomach. When Pattinson suddenly shot off through the trees, Alex knew what he was going to find.

He followed after the dog, until he found the body of Lord Daniel Cooper, lying dead at the base of a tree. He had been staked to the ground, and the blood that was seeping through the coat that lay over his chest told Mr Hunter that the young lord had been cut open.

"Stay!" Mr Hunter ordered Pattinson to guard the body whilst he went to fetch Arwyn, hoping that Lord Daniel Cooper was the Rich man and that Lady Sarah would soon be free.

Get your copy now!

About the Author

I was born in Macclesfield, Cheshire, UK, and raised in the nearby town of Wilmslow. From an early age I discovered I had a flair and passion for writing.

I began writing at the age of 7 and was first published in 2010. I currently live with my partner, Matt, and our two cats in Christchurch, New Zealand.

As an avid horsewoman and gamer, I also have a passion for singing, dancing, the theatre, and my garden.

Facebook: https://www.facebook.com/AuthorC.S.Woolley

Instagram: https://www.instagram.com/thecswoolley

Website: http://.mightierthantheswimorduk.com

Acknowledgements

Writing can be an extremely lonely profession at times, but thankfully I never have to go through any of the pressures alone. My wonderful Matthew has been a source of constant support to me during all of my writing endeavours since we first met. I couldn't ask for a more fitting partner to share my life or love with.

Writing is not something I stumbled into either, my mother, Helen, took me, and my sisters, to the library every weekend when we were young to get different books, and I always maxed out the number of books I could get. Not only did she encourage me to read, but to write as well. To say I have been writing stories and poetry since I was 7 is not an exaggeration and the development of my writing career is due in no small part to her.

My mother-in-law, Lesley, has also been a source of unflinching and unwavering support, something I could not do without.

To Laura and Sam, who have read and offered opinions, death threats and encouragement on my early drafts, you are true treasures. Amy, you too are worth your weight and more in gold for all your love and support.

It may seem that writers only function alone, but I am blessed to be part of an amazing community of authors whom I know that I have helped push me to even greater heights and success. So to Quinn Ward, Donna Higton, Charlene Perry, Scarlett Braden Moss, Bryan Cohen, Chez Churton, Eliza Green, John Beresford, Rich Cook, Robert Scanlon, Jen Lassalle, Cathy MacRae, Ariella Zoella, and Helen Blenkinsop, my dear friends, thank you.

And finally, to you, dear reader, without you there would be no books, no series, no career. I want to thank you for all the time that you spend reading my work, reviewing it, sharing it with your friends and family. Without you there would be nothing. Thank you from the bottom of my heart.

Until we meet again in my next book, thank you and adieu.

Made in the USA
Monee, IL
20 June 2022